Meet

D0715015

At

The

Wall

Wynne McCormick Ph.D.

First edition, 1995

Library of Congress Catalog Number: 93-09364

ISBN: 1-886825-00-9

Published by
The Stetson Publishing Company
Haslett, MI

Cover art by
Jackson Printing Company Inc.
Jackson, MI

Printed in the United States of America

"I found it a riveting and emotional experience—reliving all those years through your words. Because I am on active duty I cannot use my rank to endorse your outstanding book. I hope you succeed in getting the story out to as many people as possible. "

— *Vietnam Veteran*
USAF

"Wynne McCormick has given words to feelings and emotions with which many women — who were just as present to Vietnam as were the men who fought there — will readily identify.

— *Walter H. Capps*
Professor
University of California
San Diego, CA

"The tale the author tells brings home the enduring truth of war's aftermath: the pain and suffering of the relatives left behnid."

— *Edward Kaye*
Business to Business Magazine
Toronto, Canada

"The author's turmoil, even after her husband's return from Hanoi, is most akin to that of the POW/MIA families whose loved ones have not returned."

— *MIA relative*
Volunteer Coordinator
POW-MIA

"This book will do for Vietnam what M.A.S.H did for Korea."
— *Vietnam Veteran*
USAF

Acknowledgement and Appreciation
are given to:
The Michigan Council for the Arts
1988 Individual Artist's Grant

This book is dedicated
to:
POW/MIA
children, now grown,
wives,
lovers,
sisters,
brothers,
parents,
grandparents,
other relatives,
and
all friends.

Special acknowledgment is made
to:
those who, with or without choice,
have remained altogether silent
about Vietnam.

A POW/MIA 1990's Vietnam Perspective

1972: Halloween, "Peace is at Hand" by Henry Kissinger;
November, re-election of Richard Nixon as President;
December, B-52 Christmas bombings of Hanoi/Haiphong.

1973: January, Signing of Paris Peace Accords on
Vietnam; January - March, Installment return from the Gia
Lam Airport, Hanoi, North Vietnam, by reverse order of
shootdown date of 555 prisoners-of-war.

1970s: Silence on Vietnam
1980s: All-Media Hullabaloo on Vietnam
1990s: Silence on Vietnam

1994: Summer
How is it that
the Defense Department,
the Defense Intelligence Agency,
the National Security Council,
the Senate Select Committee
on POW/MIA Affairs,
the White House,
and the entire print and
television media at-large,
considered the Russian reports
of prisoners taken from Hanoi
to the Soviet Union,
such news,
when we all heard it
about the B-52 EWOs,
factual bases notwithstanding,
from the returning prisoners
who did manage to make it back,
20-plus years ago.
And
now all of our children
are grown;
every last one
is, at minimum, twenty-one.

Wanted: by the FBI and/or Vietnam Veterans Organization(s) a highly dangerous group of 555 men

<u>Failure to Appear for Arraignment regarding the following:</u>

1960s & 1970s - War Crimes: Bombings of North
Vietnam; also, upon shoot-down & capture, Inmate
Cheering in Prison Courtyards during U.S. B-52
Christmas Bombings of Hanoi

1980s - Failure to Appear in Vietnam Vets
Organization(s)

1990s - Collective Silence on Vietnam War
(note: non-MIA, non-KIA, non-female Vet,
non-nurse/paramedic Vet status)

Aliases (where known): U.S. Senators, U.S.
Vice-Presidential Candidates, NASA
astronauts

Actual Identities: U.S. Ex-Prisoners-of-(Vietnam) War

Description: White (predominant group),
Middle-Class, American, Male
Date of birth: 1934 - 1954
Citizenship: U.S.
Height &Weight: 5'7"- 6'4" & 150-220 lbs
Race: Caucasian (549), African-American (4),
Eurasian (2)

Selective Service Classification: Sp Pr (Special
Privilege) Vietnam Deferment Option (advanced
degree study, family and/or political assistance
options, e.g, President Clinton, Vice-President Quale,
professionals in science, medicine, law, etc.)

Education: minimum of Bachelor's degree

Occupation: former jet aircraft pilots (275),
crew members (co-pilots, navigators, radar
navigators, electronics warfare operators, gunners,
etc.) (280)

Marital Status: questionable (estimated
75% divorce rate)

Caution: These individuals are professionals
(Note: The Right Stuff)
physical survival skills: indoor - solitary
confinement; outdoor - tropical, Arctic, all-terrain;
collective incarceration experience 200+ years
(Hanoi Hilton, Las Vegas, The Pig Stye, The Zoo,
The Plantation, Dog Patch, others);
non-physical survival skills: silence under
torture; group tap code; math, science, literature,
history, music, art, language, chess, etc.,
course instruction from memory for prison-mates
Last Seen: White House Lawn,Washington DC, Aug. 1973,
dinner with President Nixon, Henry Kissinger,
Bob Hope, The Press, and State Dept. plus other
governmental and military dignitaries
Call or Contact: any Vietnam Vets Organ-
ization(s); Do Not Attempt To Apprehend:
due to training, "post-traumatic stress disorder(s)"
are non-options; possible approachability only
by Vietnam Veterans Organizations and/or the
American Public At-Large
Parole Violations: performance failure(s) at Vietnam
Wall — possible crew member "name rubbings"
not accomplished; possible Wall non-attendance
Names To Be Remanded Collectively:
to Vietnam Wall, to be listed with respective crew
member MIAs & KIAs, as Also Lost (unspeakable
nature of the crew member losses — collective
anguish—to be noted as mitigating circumstance
in marble postscript at Wall center)

Meet Me at the Vietnam Wall

Table of Contents

prologue

The air war over Vietnam, instigated in the Gulf of Tonkin August 4, 1964, by a single Navy jet attack on North Vietnamese torpedo boats in reprisal for an attack by the North Vietnamese on a U.S. Navy destroyer, ended as abruptly as it began, December 29, 1972, with B-52 bombing strikes over the North Vietnamese cities of Haiphong and Hanoi.

Peace talks, held in Paris between Henry Kissinger, U.S. Secretary of State, and North Vietnamese Foreign Minister, Le Duc Tho, had been discontinued at the close of the previous October. On January 11, 1973, talks were resumed, relating by all accounts to the Christmas bombing of Hanoi, and the Paris Agreement on Ending the War and Restoring Peace in Vietnam was signed January 27, 1973.

The bombing strikes were carried out by the Air Force B-52 Stratofortress bombers, with support from U.S. Air Force and Navy fighters. This series of strikes, designated Linebacker II, lasted eleven days, beginning December 18 and ending December 29. Strikes were carried out collectively by more than 100 B-52 bombers on each of the eleven nights. Initiated to shut down the flow of equipment and supplies from the North, the strikes included not only the Ho Chi Minh Trail, but such sites as railroad depots, rail lines, munition storage and supply areas, communication stations, and MIG jet airfields.

The B-52 bomber itself is a 70 ton airplane, the largest U.S. military aircraft that carries air weaponry. These include air-to-ground missiles and conventional bombs, carried by smaller aircraft as well, and they also include large nuclear weapons transported only by the B-52.

A working crew of six consists of pilot or aircraft commander, copilot, navigator, radar navigator, electronics warfare officer, and the tail gunner. Pilot, copilot, navigator, radar navigator and electronics warfare officer positions occupy a small forward compartment of the airplane, divided into three sections. In the very front, the pilot and copilot cockpit somewhat resembles that of a very large commercial aircraft in size and equipment arrangement with the exception that, unlike a passenger-carrying airliner, all five positions are fitted with equipment to jettison seats, with the crew members strapped into them, upwards from the horizontal following a forcible explosive release of overhead hatches.

The electronics warfare officer is located behind the pilot and co-pilot, also in an upward ejection seat. This position is fitted with electronic jamming equipment to counter surface to air missiles and airborne ground fire control systems, used for alerting the crew to electronic threat emissions directed toward the aircraft. Slightly behind and below the forward cockpit, a similar small compartment occupied by the navigator and radar navigator positions is designed also with adjacent seats and an instrument panel containing radar screens for navigation and bombing.

Ejection in the instances of the pilot, copilot, navigator, radar navigator and electronics warfare officer, is initiated from a manual triggering device, to the side of each seat and operated by that respective crew member. Subsequently, automatic mechanisms effect the opening at 15,000 feet of the parachutes for completion of the fall.

The tail gunner position in the very rear of the aircraft consists of a single low seat in the cone-shaped tail with quad-mounted 0.50 caliber machine guns. The seat faces the narrowed back-end of the bomber and the guns are electronically operated by the gunner whose position is one of look-out for observing visually any attacking enemy aircraft. For the purposes of bail-out in this position, the crew member, unlike the five forward crew members, must physically jump through a manually opened hatch in the base of the aircraft tail.

The middle portion of the aircraft consists of an enormous belly, hollow when emptied of ordnance; there are two small catwalks beside the central bomb bay, on opposite walls of the inside fuselage; each catwalk parallels the bomb bay of approximately 100 feet and connects the forward compartment with the rear tail gunner compartment.

The original plan for the Christmas bombings of Hanoi outlined a three-day maximum bombing of the Hanoi-Haiphong area, with three waves of B-52s to strike each night alternating with fighter coverage in daylight hours. Missions were flown above 30,000 feet, out of the range of anti-aircraft guns, but within an altitude range at which the surface-to-air missiles were most accurate. Missions were therefore flown at night to minimize visual tracking and destruction of the B-52s by the SAMs.

Bomb runs were performed in streams of twenty to thirty aircraft at at time. In the first few days of these bombings, it was thought that compression of what were termed cells or groups, composed of three bombers each within each stream of bombers, would aid in protection against SAMs and enhance electronic counter measures. This did not prove to be the case. In fact, flying in close formation was found to contribute to the vulnerability of the B-52 to SAMs, due to the very large size of the B-52 and hence its inherent maneuverability difficulties. Mission plans, which had already been extended to an eleven day period, were thus modified after Christmas.

In the original three-day plan, a general route was designated into Hanoi from the northwest. Large post-target turns were included for the purpose of B-52 removal from the range of the SAMs as quickly as possible following bomb release over designated targets; turn points were the same for each B-52. Changes in altitude and other typical maneuvering for avoiding hits by SAMs, were to be kept at a minimum due both to B-52 size and to the numbers of planes flying together. Waves or streams of three or more following the same flight path in entering and exiting the Hanoi area totaled 130 B-52s per night.

On the night of December 26, following a 36-hour lull for the Christmas Holiday, the bombing was resumed. During the lull, the word among the reconnaissance pilots was that damaged SAM sites had been restored. Due to B-52 casualties that had peaked at a loss of six B-52s in nine hours on the last night before the temporary bombing halt, U.S. Air Force flight plans were revamped to include the use of more support aircraft for strafing MIG airfields and SAM sites, and modified plans also included some variability in entering and exiting flight paths.

Bomber streams were kept compressed nevertheless, with 113 B-52 strikes occurring within 15 minutes, determined to be the most concentrated bomber attacks in the history of aerial warfare. The 15th and last B-52 was shot down, December 26th, and the final missions brought to a conclusion the Linebacker II operations without further B-52 losses, due reportedly to the destruction of Hanoi defenses.

The night of December 26, with the crew members who survived the last B-52 crash and who were captured and taken to the Hanoi Hilton, confirmation came for what the POWs living in the prison believed from the beginning of the bombing, eleven days earlier: by the tap code among prisoners, the word was disseminated that the North Vietnamese were asking for an end to the bombing and that the POWs would, in fact, be going home.

The Christmas bombings from the first day, were termed by one POW, Armageddon for the North Vietnamese.

The last B-52, lost on December 26, was hit nearly simultaneously by two, possibly three, SAMs; this B-52 was reported by those following behind in line to have burst into flame while it was still airborne. According to the same reports the hit B-52 then immediately fireballed into the ground. On board, the crew included tail gunner, Sergeant David Gavin; electronics warfare officer, Major John Dearborn; navigator, Lieutenant Michael Clark; radar navigator, Lt. Randy Smith; co-pilot, Captain Rich Cunningham; and aircraft commander, Captain Bryan Martin.

No parachutes were observed and beepers, carried by all crew members for ground rescue, were not heard. Thus, the crew as a whole was listed as missing-in-action.

1

DINNER ON THE WHITE HOUSE LAWN

DECEMBER, 1972

During Christmas week of l972, the period of then President Nixon's B-52 bombing raids on Hanoi, a conversation among my houseful of family, neighbors, and guests, ended with a consensus that my telephone was tapped. From the time of the notification of the crash, December 26, my house had been filled with Air Force officials, other B-52 crewmen, family and friends, and one day a neighbor who was answering the telephone commented on the audible interference in my telephone line, heard as intermittent clicking noises accompanied by a consistent soft-sounding static. Thereafter notes were made and comments compared about the possible tapping. Other crew member wives had noted the disturbances on their telephone lines also and collectively, we had discussed the possibility of telephone tapping. The Christmas Bombings, as they were called by the press, were a national controversy and as a consequence, the press was hounding us all for information. Perhaps tapping would provide the government with the information it needed in order to forestall a family member from speaking against President Nixon's decision to undertake it. We had no way of knowing for sure.

One late December afternoon when I was alone, I picked up the receiver, dialed 0, and waited for an operator to come on the line. I tried to imagine the paraphernalia required for tapping, and on this day, speaking very clearly into the receiver I told my tappers to be on their toes, this was the moment of the month. I asked for the Washington D.C. area code, dialed information for the Senate Office Building, and was transferred to the office of Senator Robert Mathias, Chairman of the Armed Services Committee. I was then forwarded from a series of secretaries to an aide and finally to Senator Mathias himself, all the while repeating to each new voice on the line that I was the wife of the last B-52 pilot shot down over Hanoi this week. Could I please speak with Senator Mathias concerning the pending court martial of an Air Force captain who had refused to fly the B-52 bombing raids on Hanoi, and no thank you, I did not care to divulge my name.

I could barely hear Senator Mathias, the pulse in my head was so loud. I did not want to be going public, I wasn't that bold at the moment, but I did not have the time to question my irrational thoughts about seeing myself quoted even as an Air Force pilot's wife, never mind my withholding my name, on national television on the evening news in a few hours. I stated my reason for calling.

"I'm sure you know that in the last few days there has been an incident in which a B-52 pilot has refused to fly the bombing raids on Hanoi?"

"Yes, I'm aware of that situation." I pictured Senator Mathias, whom I had seen in the media, in a Senate-like office that I had not seen.

"I realize," I went on, "That I'm hardly privy to what is going on in the bombing, that is in President Nixon's reasons for it all, but I do have some idea of what goes on among the pilots who are doing the flying."

Senator Mathias asked me to go on, saying that he wanted to know what the American public thought. What the pilots and crew members themselves thought of the situation was most assuredly of interest.

I took him at his word. "I have never actually heard any of them object to combat flying, except this time. I think that is the reason for my call. They are now talking about the fact that the bombing of Hanoi is excessively dangerous. One hundred missions a night. Fifteen B-52s are being flown in line at once and because the pilots are doing it night after night, they say the North Vietnamese know how and when they are coming. They say it's as obvious as a traffic jam. The SAMs are set in place for them. And the B-52 crews say they are sitting ducks for the SAMs."

Senator Mathias interrupted me, asking me himself if I wouldn't care to leave my name with him. I said please, no.

"If it is really important to know who I am," I said, "You'll be able to figure it out from my call. The FBI, I'm sure knows, but it wouldn't even take the FBI to do it. There are fifteen B-52s down this week, and you can identify them all. The press can do it for you. I would just rather not."

He thanked me for calling without asking more. "This is the kind of thing that we need to know," he said. "The court martial proceeding is not a certain thing." He asked if I thought the other pilots would think that pilot who had refused to fly should be court martialed. "Probably so," I said. "They don't give themselves much leeway. I would say one more thing."

"Yes, what is that?"

"They're all the same, the guys who end up going. They just do it. But the pilot I'm married to actually said two days ago that he didn't want to go back. He told me it would mean he wouldn't be coming home again. I've never heard him say, even once before in his life, that he didn't want to fly. Before the Air Force proceeds with the court martial of the captain, I think the Armed Services Committee should do some inquiring about how the flying is being conducted."

Senator Mathias assured me such an inquiry would be made, he thanked me for calling, and we concluded our conversation. I hung up disconcerted. Watching the evening news as best I could, alternately on all channels, I was greatly relieved not to see reference to my conversation with Senator Mathias.

The morning before Bryan had left, my living room had been full of B-52 pilots in the squadron at this California base in Sacramento, but it had been very quiet. There was the usual group of them and they were in flight suits now as it was a working morning. All standing, they were huddled in the sun coming through the living room length of back windows. The sun shattering the shadows of the huge Christmas tree seemed the only sound; among a group of pilots the discussion about the bombing raids on Hanoi, almost inaudible, had come to a halt: the flight plan of flying straight and level over Hanoi night after night was not acceptable — not to the least experienced, nor to the most experienced, Vietnam pilot.

AUGUST, 1973

Perhaps I should say it straight out now: I am the ex-wife of an ex-POW, Mrs. Ex-Ex-POW, as it were. My former husband was B-52 aircraft commander, Bryan Martin.

This all started on Halloween, October, 1972, and moved more swiftly than we could keep pace with: Henry Kissinger, then Secretary of State, that day made the announcement, "Peace is at Hand," stating that negotiations with both South and North Vietnam were pending. The American public was hardly credulous. On November 8th, Richard Nixon was re-elected President, and in December, the bombing of Hanoi was instigated for two weeks, and just as quickly, it was stopped. The Paris Peace Accord was signed January 11, and the release of the POWs began February 11, 1973, and ended March 30, 1973. Again, no one paid much attention to the politics. For all of the arrangements that Secretary Kissinger presented regarding the withdrawal of our troops plus the taking over of the fighting by South Vietnamese troops, we knew better. We were finally calling it a day in Vietnam.

That next August it was dinner for all POW families on the White House lawn. I had refused to go, I couldn't exactly say why, but Bryan had said he just had to talk to Henry Kissinger himself about the MIAs. He said he had something to say to Richard Nixon as well.

Ex-Pows and their wives, girl friends, or mothers were flown to Washington, where all were to stay in downtown Washington hotels, then to be bussed the evening of the dinner to the White House. In the lobby, where people were collecting in the early evening to be loaded onto the buses, Bryan pointed out some famous POWs who, he said, had been held captive for many years, and in turn, became heroes to the incoming captives. He was pointing now to the two longest-held POWs: one, a Navy pilot, Admiral Stockdale, had been the the commander of all the camps. Bryan said that he had never met him before and that he was glad to have come just to meet him in person.

From the bus ride downtown, we were dropped at the White House gate where we lined up out the front door and down the walk to shake hands with Henry Kissinger and other State Department dignitaries, who stood for greetings just inside. Our welcome by President Nixon would come after dinner. From the White House we were ushered through a tent tunnel onto the front lawn which was elaborately set for a reception of the POWs and their families, some 1000 people, for a Welcome Home Dinner.

In six hours' time after our leaving California we were stepping through the end of a long green and white striped canvas tunnel from White House to White House lawn. The makeshift tunnel itself was unlighted: through Blue Room lights from the White House on one end and the blinding lights of camera flash bulbs from the other, we saw our way through the middle of the tunnel. It was already dark. One could see that there were more green and white striped awnings out on the lawn. We were being photographed and televised as we had been for months. Stepping from the tunnel's end, there was little room to move: a collection of photographers and reporters surrounded the opening beyond which we were to find assigned tables for dinner.

"I thought you said this POW was coming with a Playboy Bunny," I heard as I looked into the cameras at the tunnel's opening onto the lawn and felt my feet find the grass. I can barely see through the lights, but I figure it out fast; it is one disappointed reporter talking to another.

"That's what I heard. It's on the roster," was the response of the second. Even though it was too bright to see either of them, simultaneously with the reporters' and photographers' mistakes, I realized they were talking about me. According to the guest roster, I was to have been the Playboy Bunny.

I smiled brilliantly. "Sorry," I spoke into the air, "Try the next one." I looked in the direction of the voices and then reflexively back over my shoulder, half expecting to see someone in a Bunny Suit.

The White House lawn swelled with circular tables of white linen, perhaps l00 of them; there were as many black-tuxedoed waiters as tables, and there were flood lights on top of flash bulbs, television camera lights on top of flood-lights. The momentary blindings of lights were real enough, now and then throughout the evening.

I see General Scowcroft, then Henry Kissinger's stand-in on the National Security Council when Henry was out of the country, as Mrs. Scowcroft put it, and Chairman of the National Security Council in the Bush Administration. I see him without watching him, across the table from me, watching me as I tacitly refuse to participate in the evening's festivities. His disapproval is apparent even in my peripheral vision. I consider a trip to the Ladies Room to cinch it, an excuse to stand up so General Scowcroft can confirm that my presence is definitely desultory. I don't know why, but I don't want to be here.

I have on maroon-black roses top to toe, the closest thing to a long gown, but in fact, not a gown. If I walk, it will be apparent that I am wearing pants, my waist length pearls, notwithstanding, a means of making sure I would be noticeable; I am, in fact, six feet tall, there is also that. It matters little, now or then, but I had dressed purposefully ignoring what I had thought of as a White House edict, a directive I wish that I had, in fact, saved; it instructed all women to wear long gowns: wives, girl friends, mothers of ex-POWs, because President Nixon, it said, *preferred women in dresses*. Even the Playboy Bunny must have worn a dress. But I sit tight and look straight at General Scowcroft, sitting against a creamy white rectangle of light, the White House behind him, its lighted windows, creamier still in the black sky. One imagines easily the days of Dolly Madison when the White House burned and she carried, in a horse-drawn carriage, as many paintings as she could manage across the Potomac to safety. General Scowcroft's outline, at our table of eight, is a shadowgram. I imagine President Lincoln, President Franklin Roosevelt, President John Kennedy, and I try to remember who was President Kennedy's Secretary of State, and who was his Secretary of State's closest assistant?

Mrs. Scowcroft, a soft, plump, and pleasant lady, talks of nothing but the General, as she calls him, our perfunctory introductions having been made: General and Mrs. Scowcroft, Captain and Mrs. Mayberry, Major and Mrs. Dearborn, Bryan and myself at this circular table of eight. The conversation has to do with the General's serving as stand-in for Henry Kissinger this past week-end. He apparently has a secure telephone on which he talks exclusively with Secretary Kissinger. I wonder, idly, if a secure telephone has an unusual appearance. Although I make an honest effort at conversation, averting a more lengthy discussion on the security of telephones, it is obvious at least to me, and I know to Bryan, that the General and I are not getting on well together. Bryan, smiling continuously, is enjoying it thoroughly.

I turn to the couple next to me and hear myself saying to Major Dearborn who is directly on my left, that the MIA member of Bryan's crew was also a Major Dearborn and was he himself an ex-POW?

His ruffled shirt and unusual tux, and the lack of any name tag belied this possibility, as a mess dress is in order for Air Force crew members, ribbons, medals, and all. I look at Bryan who is grinning still. He is lucky to have his mess dress on since it was at the cleaners still this morning when, an hour before the flight was to leave, we had finally agreed together to go.

As it was we were half an hour late due to a traffic jam on the freeway to the Sacramento airport, both of us, I thought, even though we wouldn't have admitted it, relieved to have had the decision about going finally settled. It did not occur to us that the flight would be held for the half hour that we were delayed. It was therefore no wonder that we were surprised by a United Airlines official at the curb who, opening the car door as swiftly as Bryan put on the brakes, asked if we were Captain and Mrs. Martin? He knew who we were, where we were going, this airline official, and he had held the flight thirty minutes, with no idea that we would, in fact, arrive.

Now it is barely six hours later. Not to my surprise, Major Dearborn says "No." He is not an ex-POW. Not another word. Sitting next to him, I try not to stare at him sideways. The only evidence of his even being a Major Dearborn at all is the place setting name card I am looking at on the table. The conversation returns to General Scowcroft's activities, his recent involvement in keeping the country running while Henry Kissinger has been in negotiations and in his reminiscences of West Point. It turns out that the father of Captain Mayberry, another B-52 pilot seated to the right of Bryan and appearing younger even than Bryan, also went to West Point and played football there a few years later than the General. The conversation lags as we exhaust the topic of West Point.

"You know," I go on, wondering if the whole evening will be spent in small talk with not one query, question, or comment, from General Scowcroft about their experiences to these B-52 pilots — perhaps the General felt upstaged by a tableful of Distinguished Flying Crosses, Purple Hearts, what-have-you — "I remember seeing on television at the time that the POWs were released and taken to the Philippines, a huge poster in the crowd of people at Clark Air Force Base, saying 'Welcome Home, Major

Dearborn.'

"At first I thought that it was a miracle, that somehow in the release of prisoners from Hanoi, the man we knew as Major Dearborn on Bryan's crew, whom the North Vietnamese had indicated to Bryan they had either dead or alive, was, in fact, alive and being released. I thought maybe I just had not gotten the word. I hadn't talked to Bryan then yet, or to Major Dearborn's wife that day.

"I wondered then who was the Major Dearborn for whom that poster was made, and just now it occurred to me when we were introduced that it might have been you."

There was no comment from him. It was as though I hadn't spoken. His wife had told me he was stationed at Fort Ord, which I knew to be an intelligence base, and having decided that he was not a pilot, I concluded that he must be, in fact, an intelligence officer. Perhaps he was seated next to me because the government knew that I had called Senator Mathias about the court martial of the B-52 pilot. But that didn't make sense either, for we wouldn't have been seated at General Scowcroft's table if anyone was really concerned about what I would say.

I cease thinking, cease trying to figure it all out. The shadows deepen, and I sink back into them. The conversation goes on without me. Who was it who brought the evening's entertainment? John Wayne, Bob Hope, or Jimmy Stewart? I can see the stage again, a huge platform beyond the awnings, far out on the grass, but who is on it is completely unclear. During it, I find the General's attention directed towards me as I continue to stare at the stage set-up on the White House lawn. In fact, I can imagine that he is glaring at me. I return his look unflinchingly, and simultaneously I realize that a nearby television camera is pointing, blindingly, straight in my direction. I turn my head. Now I know what it is that has bugged me all along about coming. It is the darkened holes in the evening. For me it is the wrong Major Dearborn in the adjacent seat. Beyond the perimeter of lights, moving as steadily as if mounted on a glittering amusement park carousel, out in the land, the families of those who didn't come back, they are watching all those lights on their darkened televisions. Those of the killed and missing in action. Finally it is clear to me: all of us families, POW/MIA, should have stayed together in whatever we did. Either all of us — or none of us — should have come.

2

THE UNDERGRADUATES: BEFORE THE AIR FORCE

The fall of 1963, after the summer that I met Bryan in my hometown of West Lafayette, Indiana, my middle sister Colleen was starting her second year at the University of Michigan, and Bryan and I took her to Ann Arbor. Our parents were away for the year, so Bryan and I were going to install her as another of my friends termed it; he had two younger sisters and was familiar with the whole routine of moving one's sister back and forth from college. Amidst Colleen's stuff for dorm living jammed into the station wagon, we had packed needed equipment for camping on Lake Michigan on our way past Chicago, to Ann Arbor.

The three of us had spent a lot of time together that summer. At the beginning of the summer I had, in fact, tried to fix Bryan and Colleen up on a date with each other; I talked sometimes incessantly about each to the other in my effort. In that first week before she had met him Colleen had asked "If you think he's so neat, why don't you go out with him yourself?"

"Because he's too short and too young for me," was my response. In those college days, both seemed like real questions. "For me, he's as much shorter than I as you are. That's too much." We were talking four or five inches. We all had summer lab jobs at Purdue University. Bryan, from Ft. Wayne, Indiana, was an undergraduate staying at Purdue through the summer: for both Bryan and Colleen it was a first summer in a research lab, but for me it was the interim between my first two years of medical school and my fourth summer lab job .

Colleen was working in the Biochemistry Department, a building or two away from the Life Sciences building where Bryan and I worked, so when it wasn't too hot the three of us ate our sack lunches together sometimes midway between; or we ate in the one of our labs, when air conditioning seemed a necessity.

Bryan had received an undergraduate National

Science Foundation grant to work in the laboratory of Michael Rossman, who was on his way to becoming a renowned X-ray crystallographer. His lab in the Department of Biological Sciences was in the sub-basement of a monstrous building, and the whole floor seemed rather like a subway labyrinth both in the moldiness of the air and in the low ceiling of rows of flat fluorescent bulbs that didn't really light up the place. The lab itself was bare of equipment at the time that I met Bryan. Even then, before Michael had made the name that may bring him a Nobel Prize in the not too distant future, Purdue knew a good thing in Michael Rossman, enticing him to come from England. And he was the very image back then of a brilliant mad scientist. Listening to him, I always had difficulty not staring at his hair, which seemed to turn in an even swirl clockwise around his head.

This was the summer of Michael's setting up his laboratory. My summer's project was the purification of the crystalline form of LDH, Lactic Dehydrogenase, a ubiquitous enzyme that could apparently be crystallized most easily from yeast. Michael had given me a paper with a protocol for the making of LDH crystals from baker's yeast, which I would use as a starting point for my summer's project. And Bryan had been hired to do the computer programming for the X-ray crystallographic structure study of proteins, starting with LDH. They were the days when Purdue's only computer was housed in the engineering building. There the computer took up the whole first floor of the building, its enormity glassed-in completely with a circumferential path at the building's walls, due to special heating and air conditioning arrangements that had to be made for it. Daily, Bryan walked back and forth to drop off and pick up programs and data: personal computers and pocket calculators hadn't been invented yet.

In the lab, Bryan's desk was next to mine. Michael introduced us there, and we talked after he left the room about what a virtually empty lab this seemed to be. It was, we knew, to be shared between Michael and another faculty member, Ed McGandy, whom Bryan came to admire as much as he did Michael. There were three or four other desks in this room, but as yet, he and I were apparently the only occupants. The working laboratory next door was equally empty and in rudimentary working form: lab benches and a few pieces of large equipment constituted the set-up so far for this research lab. Although by the end of the summer it would be full both of Englishmen and Americans, gathered by Michael and Ed, there were no other students, technicians, or post-docs, presently working. For the moment, Bryan and I were the sole occupants of this X-ray crystallographic lab.

The first day of work as I was on my way out the door to walk to my dad's office across campus, Bryan offered me a ride home. He said he had a new Corvette and had just figured out that we lived a block apart. It would be easy to drop me off.

I said, "Sure," called my dad's office to say I had a ride home, and we headed up the two flights of steps from the sub-basement to the back of the building.

Outside I looked around for what he had said was a green Corvette when he said to me, "Here it is." I looked. He was getting onto a green Schwinn bike in a rack right beside the door to the building.

Not to be outdone, I commented, "Oh, that's nice," standing there, wondering what next, and he then suggested that I get on — the middle bar — if I didn't mind a bumpier ride than I had anticipated.

I said, "Why not?" He had already said he lived near my house, I couldn't imagine where, but I was curious. I didn't say anymore while I balanced myself on the bar and he started off pedaling across campus.

Midway, I asked him point blank, "So you actually live on my same street?" We'd stopped off to eat in the village next to campus.

"That's right. I live at the Green Door."

I tried not to look surprised. This summer I was living at home with my parents, up the hill from where he was staying. I knew all about it. It was a Sigma Chi fraternity apartment, in a house down the hill. Since we'd been kids, junior high age, my friend Julie, who lived two houses away from it, and I had heard and known of the Green Door.

In those days, we'd sat on the stone embankment along her driveway, wondering by the hour, among other things, what went on down there: the Green Door was an apartment in the basement of a neighbor's house, a private residence, two doors down from Julie's house, and between the garage and the breezeway, the apartment door entrance was actually painted green.

The Sigma Chis rented it year-round. In high school, Julie and I and all of our buddies had watched the fraternity guys come and go, but we had never even spoken to any of what were taboo college guys for us as high school town girls.

There was definitely some humor in it now. Junior high and high school were in the past; in college Julie and I had gone beyond what we considered playboy college boys, like the Sigma Chis, we were sure of that. Julie had recently met Brage, a physics major and jazz pianist who was going to MIT to graduate school; they had met at a fraternity jam session where she was singing and he was playing piano. I was dating a physics grad student at Purdue.

We had both graduated from college the summer before. But I would probably, for old times' sake call her and tell her we might get a chance to see the Green Door, just for the fun of it, at long last. If I could fix Colleen up with Bryan.

On the ride home Bryan rode up my street past the Green Door and Julie's house at the bottom of the hill, then on up to my house. It was a two-block hill, steep enough to be blocked off for sledding in the winters, and without dumping me off, Bryan stood up to pedal up the hill. He let me off, I thanked him for the ride, and he took off flying down the hill no-handed and disappeared into the driveway of the Green Door: watching him, I wished for a second time in one week that he were taller and older.

That's how it all got started with Bryan and me. It began very simply. The next week he took me motorcycle riding on the river road south of town. At work, I would walk to the bakery, some 8-10 blocks into the village off-campus, to buy what were brick-sized blocks of baker's yeast, which I would then mash and use for the purification of the enzyme, and Bryan began going with me, his excuse being that he had to stop off at the computer center. Besides, he told me, he could work anywhere, even while he was walking.

We would stop often, either coming or going, at the drug store in the village next to the campus where I learned of the myriad things he had done already in his life. At Arth's Drug Store they still served cherry cokes at an old-fashioned fountain in the back and as the overhead fan droned, he told me on one of those days that he wanted to be an astronaut. I thought he would probably do it and Purdue — this school, enormous of itself, but dwarfed in its reputation in other academic areas by its engineering school — had already produced the beginning of its string of astronaut graduates then. Among other things, Bryan told me he had gone mountain climbing in Switzerland, run the Bull Runs in Spain, eaten a goat's eye with villagers in Yemen, and he said had a Masai spear given to him by villagers in Africa.

Not until a year later when I told him that I had gone to see Mont Blanc, the mountain I thought he had climbed in Switzerland, did it become truly believable. I told him I had taken a cog train up Mont Blanc, just to see it, and while I was describing it, he matter-of-factly informed me that I had gone up the wrong mountain. It was the Jungfrau that he had climbed. He had climbed the Jungfrau instead of the Matterhorn when he was in Switzerland, at sixteen with his dad, because the Matterhorn had been closed that day.

By the end of the summer after countless trips to the bakery, I had accomplished the extraction LDH in crystalline form. I was a bit incredulous myself. Bryan and I were trading back and forth with each other at the microscope looking at them: visible under low power, they looked like tiny pieces of cut glass, produced to the surprise of us all, from the gray, sticky blocks of baker's yeast that I had spent my summer with. Now it was August. Michael was clearly pleased as he looked up from the microscope, calling Ed and the rest in to look. Then I looked again to see these diamond-like tiny cubes, that had emerged from a mixture that started with the feel of putty, turning into a worse mixture that was gooey, bad-smelling, and almost intractable to work with before becoming this: amazingly, a set of colorless crystals of a single protein.

I had begun, with Bryan's help, by piecing together equipment from within the department and setting up new equipment as it came in. His single piece of equipment for the summer for X-ray crystallographic analysis didn't come in until the end of the summer; so, while doing his preliminary programming, Bryan was helping me out. One piece of equipment I knew could not be ordered from a catalog was a ceramic ball mills, specified in the paper I used as a crystallization protocol. In stainless steel I might find something comparable, but for use with yeast it needed to be ceramic. I was having difficulty coming up with options for dispersing the yeast into solution.

One afternoon, having been gone for quite awhile, Bryan showed up with what looked like a huge cookie jar; it was ceramic. I smiled at what I knew was to be my ball mills for this purification procedure. He had found it in the back of a storeroom. It fit on its own stand sideways, with large screws to hold it on either end and to hold the top on tight. We plugged it partially full with mashed up yeast in the cold room, where we had set it up for shaking at 4 degrees centigrade, and checked all the bolts. Then we turned it on and took off together. It was to shake overnight.

The next morning, opening the cold room door, I found a nasty note directing the parties using the ball mills to clean the mess up fast: it was placed on top of a pile of broken pieces of ceramic; the balls mills had apparently busted during the night, spraying yeast all over the cold room. Compared to the lab equipment in the department, it had looked archaic, but it clearly had been well-used before this and the stand and brace were sturdy for holding and shaking it. Setting the apparatus on the floor of what was a small, closet-sized cold room, we had concluded that its breaking was unlikely. But we had not thought of a potential risk in its breaking, aside from making a mess, that we had to consider now. The shelves of the small room were arranged neatly with the cultures of Seymour Benzer, Purdue's most famous biologist. Now, particles of mashed yeast were visible both on the floor and on the nearby shelves: the tacit gist of the anonymous note had to do with our possibly having contaminated Dr. Benzer's cultures with yeast. In fact, our breaking the ball mills might have gone unnoticed, or at least uncommented upon, had the cultures belonged to anyone but Seymour Benzer.

At the speed of kids who had set a prank, we had the cold room cleaned in no time and then were on our way to the bakery to buy more yeast, figuring how, as we went, we would rig up the smashing of the yeast this time, and deciding perhaps we should talk to Dr. Benzer, or at least to Michael, about it. We weren't anxious to undo what we knew to be rather incredible molecular genetics studies of the already famous Seymour Benzer.

At the end of the summer the week-end that we were going to take Colleen back to school, the three of us had decided we would camp on our way to Ann Arbor. We finally got going late Friday afternoon to head north toward Chicago, all of us looking forward to camping on Lake Michigan.

We joked about having much too much paraphernalia for a one-night campout — in weather that was almost still summery. Bryan had an arctic sleeping bag made mummy-style, wide at the top and narrowing to the toes, visibly tight, and it was down-lined. We also had his two-man tent, which after we had it pitched, Bryan said would be for Colleen and me while he used the sleeping bag, and we had a whole array of cooking utensils plus a favorite compass of Bryan's, lanterns, and rafts for swimming.

We by-passed Chicago, turning just south of the city and following the heat-simmered trail of Indian Summer diagonally up and across Indiana into Michigan. Then we headed east along the lake front highway toward the Michigan Dunes State Park. We found a camping spot close to the water and starting unpacking, talking about what we had brought along for eating and sleeping. We decided to go swimming first before building a campfire for a cookout. In the dusk we cooked what became a mountain of food for the three of us; the campsite appeared to be deserted with the exceptions of ourselves. Summer was at an end: the sun went down on just the three of us and we filled up the air with our own talk about everything that came to mind and then about the upcoming year for us each.

In the night we all awakened to a torrential rain, so Bryan piled into the tent with Colleen and me, all of us on top of the crackling leaves still dry in the rain; we had seen and felt them already coming down in the wind before the rain, in flocks; fall was on its way, and we talked in the dark, above the noise of the rain on the tent, for a long while about various courses we had taken and were planning to take, and then about college majors as Bryan was in the midst of changing his from biology to chemistry and Colleen needed to decide hers soon; she was saying she thought she would major in botany. I lay there thinking about being an undergrad again. I had majored in chemistry, the very last subject I would have picked for myself until I settled on it. I had always thought Colleen had rather more of a natural bent for science than I. So, majoring in any science could have made sense, I thought, for her.

Yearly she had been growing squash, gourds, and such in our backyard at home, huge beige and gold ones, ludicrously speckled some of them. I got sick of having them around all over the place, but I did love the colors, I remembered the pale lime-green and chocolate brown ones the best, year to year. They would grow in the back yard, mysteriously planted before the winter was over; then they would move inside in the fall, full-grown.

At home, we all had walked around them lined up on the back porch. I could remember eating some few of them, and then the rest would disappear as mysteriously unnoticed as they had appeared. The next year the growing would start all over again. A major in botany made sense. More sense than my majoring in chemistry, and I had liked it well enough.

The next day we found Jordan Hall on a good-sized hill above the University of Michigan tennis courts. It was on the stick of a lollipop-shaped drive that ran along the edge of the hill and which, on the loop of it, housed the university hospitals. The drop-off to the tennis courts behind the dorm was so steep that you could see clear sky through the windows opposite the main entrance of the dorm, and the trees that day, every one in the row on the drive, were washed-down gold: you could see through the leaves as clearly as you could see through the dorm windows. Over and down the hill.

Jordan Hall was one in a pair of narrow rectangular buildings which sat on a high spot in Ann Arbor. It was, in fact, ivy-covered. Both dorms seemed just barely balanced on the embankment. Colleen's room was on the top floor. She knew from checking in at the desk that her roommate was already there, and we went on up.

Bryan turned around the room. It seemed bare to all of us. We were thinking the same thing, simultaneously, the three of us. Her roommate, whoever she was, had staked herself out at the best dresser, bed, and desk; none of us would take exception to that. It was dorm living.

He said it — the other thing we all were thinking: "She doesn't have any books." Not one.

"I know." Colleen was peering around the corner into the bathroom, as though to make one last check for a book of some sort somewhere. She didn't say more.

"She's short," I said, now in a semi-disparaging assessment. I could tell it from her clothes and shoes, which I didn't like, but their lack of appeal had little enough to do with her height. Just clothes I, and no one I knew, would ever buy. She was from New York. For the moment it was becoming an unsavory place. The East and the Midwest were being gyroscoped into their farthest polarities in the same moment, and I was glad for once we, collectively, were midwesterners. It was the brush and comb that were the give-away of an even greater differentness — ugly and dirty — both of them, never mind whatever affluence she came with, although that part was also somewhat different. I imagined her to be short and dark, unfamiliar, and the opposite of Colleen, my tall blond sister to whom, clearly, I would remain partial. I did not run down the hall, yelling for a new roommate for my sister; but I would have called out for anyone to do. Last year there had been three roommates, two in a row quitting school altogether during the year, and the third never returned for a second year. That was the least anyone could do for someone who was going to college, give them a decent roommate one of those years: make a trade of one unseen roommate for another; it didn't matter at this point. I looked around and down the hall, wondering if the real one would appear before we unpacked, hoping simultaneously that she would and would not, show up.

We all hurried to dump Colleen's things, so we could get out of there, and get back into the old station wagon to drive around Ann Arbor and put off our parting. But we knew Colleen would be OK, despite any roommate. It wasn't a big deal anyway; she had a good schedule of courses and we could even be surprised about her roommate. Colleen was taking two German Literature courses, and we had all discussed the molecular biology course she was taking. She was also signed up for a course in limnology, a subject in biological science I had not known existed. Bryan made out that he knew all about it, and listening to him describe its contents, both Colleen and I laughed. We were beginning to know him. His smile, when he was telling stories, was becoming recognizable. For now, Colleen and I just had each other and Bryan: our parents, out of the country for a year, wouldn't be back until the coming September. I would also call Brage when I returned home to tell him we had installed Colleen just fine at the University of Michigan.

We headed out of the dorm to find a place to eat: in a corner drugstore Bryan bought a copy of The Hobbit off the rotating book rack. No one had heard of it then. Colleen and I bought Mademoiselle and Glamour magazines and went up and down the shops of State Street next to campus. The September heat was affixed to the sidewalks for the remainder of the late afternoon, refusing to turn cool. We nevertheless talked of skirts and sweaters, jeans, and dressy dresses for fall and winter, going from store to store, while Bryan sat in the car and started in on his find of The Hobbit. Finally, we had to drop Colleen off back at the dorm — and next, back at Purdue, while I packed my stuff in an afternoon at home to go back to medical school in Indianapolis — Bryan settled himself for a few hours to read The Hobbit; finishing it, he went out to an all night grocery and bought the three-book set of the Lord of the Rings Trilogy to bury himself in before school started, for the time, in the Green Door.

3

THE JUST MARRIED: PRE-VIETNAM

The winter of his senior year at Purdue, 1967, Bryan and I got married. All started out innocently enough; neither of us had much in the way of fortitude for going through with a wedding so we arranged it, by tacit agreement, in his threatening to join the Marines if I didn't marry him in two weeks and my consenting to believe him. I didn't wear a white dress and we had it at home.

I moved into the Green Door which seemed ludicrous. Bryan's roommate had graduated mid-year; this was February and the Sigma Chis who were apparently tolerating Bryan's past nonparticipation by not kicking him out altogether, agreed to it; moreover, he became somewhat of a legend, maverick-like, for getting away with it. No one except the seniors even knew him. He was both a member and a non-member.

The preceding year, my second year of medical school, I had decided that medicine — big biology as I called it — was not it for me. Still at Indiana University and after many changes of mind, plus a suggested leave of absence for a year from the Dean, should I change my mind once more, I was now enrolled in the Ph.D. program in biochemistry. It wouldn't make much difference now. I was quitting and taking a Master's to get married.

Three weeks later, the first week in March, my parents had a wedding reception at home for Bryan and me, delayed for those weeks because our shot-gun like wedding had left little time for planning for anything except getting married. My father had set Sunday, March 5, a week-end when Colleen would be home on Spring break from the University of Michigan, for the reception.

That day Bryan looked great in navy blue suit which until this day I had seen only in closets; the living room was packed with more people than my mother had expected, some of whom I knew, many of whom I did not: colleagues of my father's, the family dentist and doctor, the high school principal, my piano teacher, Bryan's mother and friends of hers from around the state, neighbors, and more. Over Bryan's shoulder, I can see all of my home town: our house is on the main hill of West Lafayette. This is central Indiana. There is another hill, across town, as we always say, with the Wabash River running in the trough between.

Colleen is leaving to catch a flight back to school. It has started to snow, and collectively Bryan, Colleen, and I look up the Lake Central Airlines number to make sure they are flying today. They say yes, and Colleen makes a trip upstairs for her bag and books. Bryan and I are to pick the car up at the Purdue Airport after the party. I hurry out of the living room, still full of guests, to walk out to the car with her. She and I hug and agree upon looking forward to seeing each other again soon, since school at the University of Michigan would be out in another month or so and Purdue would still be in session then. We would still be in town.

In the evening Bryan and I have gone back to the Green Door, down the hill from my own house, and I lay back on a bunk bed to think about the day. Out of the blue, there seems to be some commotion on the steps. I look at my watch. It is just 11:15. Not being a real Sigma Chi apartment at the moment, it strikes us both as odd: then comes a sound of hysterics of some sort on the steps and a pounding on the door.

Bryan lets in my own mother in her pajamas and coat. Her voice says it, even though I am in the bedroom and never heard it that first time: Colleen is dead. Colleen has been killed in an airline crash. She is moving about the room somehow. I have come out of the bedroom. I walk back into it, just large enough for the bunk bed I have been lying on and with barely enough space between the bunk and the wall to walk beside it.   Bryan is in that space telling me my mother says Colleen is dead. I don't remember how the three of us all got back up the hill. I presume we ran up as she had run down.

"We have to call someone, the airlines. We have to ask," I managed to say aloud, "If they know, for sure, that she's really dead. We have to hurry up and go there, Kenton, Ohio, wherever that is, maybe she's not dead yet."

My mother says they had told her that the plane had broken in half and crashed in seconds on a farm near Kenton, Ohio. "They said everyone was dead, the pilot and stewardesses, and all the passengers." She is incredulous.

I ignored it: what if we could get to that farm fast enough to keep her from freezing to death, that would be the trick. It had been snowing all night since the party. Now it was l AM. But it was clear that it was at least a three hour drive to Kenton, Ohio, to this farm. My dad has a map out. Kenton was in the northern part of Ohio. We were in the middle of Indiana. We would go by way of Ft. Wayne, Bryan's hometown, to get there.

Our family doctor shows up just as we pile into the car, my parents, Bryan, Monica, my youngest sister, and I. We drop Monica off at a friend's house; my parents think she is too young to go through this. By this time it is going on 2 AM, and the snow is falling in great huge bundles out of the pitchblack, soft on the windshield, obscuring the view even with the wipers going full-blast, but not slippery, only soft, under the wheels. I can feel us not slipping. My father is driving with Bryan ready to switch off with him, and my mother and I are in the back seat.

Riding, I imagine Colleen in various positions on the ground in the snow amid airplane parts: two big pieces we were told about and some smaller ones. Is she still strapped in her seat, I wonder — what awful places the mind has to go — or is she out of her seat flat in the snow? Is anyone else near her? Is she crying ? In the pitch black of a snow-white night. The farmer must have called the State Police, if it really happened. While I had been lying on my bunk thinking she was in Ann Arbor in her dorm room, she had been lying in the snowy field: I hadn't gotten it right.

The end of the trip I cannot recall, exactly. By the time we arrived at the town of Kenton, Ohio, it was daylight. Sure enough, there was an airliner in two huge pieces. From the fence I was afraid to look. We had been told the bodies were cleared from the field.

We went to a church that was now a temporary morgue. They said the bodies were in the church basement. My parents and Bryan and I sat in a last row of chairs against the back wall, not a pew, but a row of folding chairs. The pews themselves were scattered with people. Arrangements were made between my father and someone who stood at the end of the last pew, for going down to identify Colleen's body. Bryan has his arm on my mother's shoulder; he urges her to sit. I sit also. My eyes meet his; this is not our usual dare to each other. The answer is clear. I will let him go for me. I feel his eyes still on me, my own looking elsewhere. I know better than to be ashamed, but I am — of my lack of courage. He and my father leave for the church's basement steps, and I walk strangely down the aisle to where the piano is at the altar. I sit and wonder, while I play my favorite Brahms Waltz, where on the floor down there she is.

We drove the 250-odd miles home and stopped at a cafeteria in Logansport, Indiana, on our way. We were nearly home, and it was nearly evening. The sun was setting over the main street buildings of this town, so close to my own, but familiar only in this main street through it and in its basketball and football teams from high school. Darkness was coming down on the street: yellow-orange lights from inside filled the cafeteria windows, one huge bright square in this darkening block-large building of apartments, offices, and street-front stores.

Except for the cafeteria, all the businesses were closed for the day. The March setting sun may have fallen into the building itself. Stopping for a dinner meal was no stranger than the opening or closing of the car door: now it was an interim between car door closings.

I noticed in the ensuing days that the town ladies measured our taking it, as was said, by how many bites of the many meals they fixed for days, that we each ate. Being able to eat was not the question: my question as I sat in front of my cafeteria tray wondering if the sun had set regularly or had, in fact, dropped into the pit of this building, was how did it come about that I was here, while she was there, my sister — flat on a church floor — waiting to be transported to a funeral parlor in Kenton, Ohio, and then to be picked up by us in a Lafayette funeral parlor hearse, to be transported back here, embalmed, and then transported to Indianapolis to be cremated. I sense that my heart is about to be seared. Whether or not the sun has fallen into this building.

The thought of Colleen in ashes is inconceivable. The idea of keeping her intact in embalming fluid is not an improvement. It makes me want to throw up. Bryan is holding my hand under the table, squeezing it hard. The sky is completely dark now outside in the street: the yellow-orange square of the cafeteria light makes a frame in reverse, now of the empty street. We will have to get up and go out in a few minutes.

Dear Colleen:
Blood of my blood, flesh of my flesh, you are/were/are my sister. Your body is almost as familiar to me as my own: you — tall, blond and beautiful, and I — taller still, a bunch of different hair colors, auburn if one word is necessary: they never called me beautiful, but striking they did. Our eyes, I think were always close to the same pale color and in our brains we were nearly interchangeable: you would have had to learn to argue somewhat more vehemently and I would have had to learn to be quieter and to speak German. Somehow when we were together, we were both beautiful; people would stare: I remember the summer in Europe, and we would play on our resemblance to each other, bending our heads together, arm in arm, as sisters do in Italy until they would ask if we weren't sisters ourselves. When we were apart it wasn't the same, neither a real beauty, just tall and OK enough looking, like anyone else. Now that you are gone, I am just lost. The sun has fallen into my own heart. I am about to know that every day for the rest of my life.

The only thing I remember between trips to Kenton, Ohio, was picking up my uncle at an airport; he had flown in from Oregon and would drive us back to Kenton where we were to come for Colleen's body. We drove there again at night and spent the night at a motel. I lay on the bed staring at the ceiling, turning finally, to Bryan, wishing for my own hysterics. We arose and went to the place they said to come, where they brought out Colleen's body on a regular stretcher with an Army-like blanket over it. You could see the form of a body underneath. Bryan was holding my arm this time. And so the terror, already set in, solidified itself.

All those steps of grief they talk about. They are pure baloney in comparison with this, the preface to grief, pure unparalleled terror. Daylight hours you've known your whole life, supplanted, and with a simple sight that is transfigured beyond belief.

I didn't know whether to rush to the stretcher and rip off the blanket and prove them all wrong, the airline and FAA officials, the FBI, the State Police, the farmer and minister, the whole pack of them; whether to walk up and lift it gently, so I wouldn't have to see her and just climb in next to her; or whether to get into the hearse so that the plexiglas partition between the back and front would somehow spare me from becoming crazed.

I rode with my glance askance most of the time, as though to look off at the scenery, riding between my mother and the hearse driver, when in reality I was looking sideways at the back, at Colleen closer to me than she was when we lay in our beds in the dark at home, talking and laughing into the night.

Sometimes I would just turn and stare, waiting for her to move and waken, don't kid yourself: waiting, turned back again to the scenery, out of the corner of my eye, the very white of it, to absorb the endlessness of that terror.

4

A FIRST AIR CRASH

Auntie Fessner sits, as always, in her high-backed winged chair, in the corner opposite her front door surrounded by her stacks of books: she is like a grandmother to me, only perhaps more regal in appearance, somehow always in repose. This is something possibly coincident with the fact of her knees being so swollen with arthritis that walking is nearly impossible and that she is almost always in her chair, where we all visit her. Rarely, in her latter years, did we see her walk, even the short distances around downstairs.

She made the steps to the second floor in the evening, the one time a day, a set of incredibly steep and twisting steps. They seemed to go almost vertically up, and they were very narrow, barely wider than she herself, in that huge house of either three or four stories, I never knew which, of antique brick.

Despite the many times of my childhood and teenage years that I had visited Auntie Fessner, either in the company of my mother or of my sisters, often carrying something special for her from my mother, I had only once seen her bedroom. It had been a time I spent a few days with her when my parents were away for a year, and the house was rented. I had needed a place to stay, one time my second year of medical school.

Somehow, her life seemed as much of a mystery as well. Thomas Fessner, her husband, taught theology at a seminary in Chicago, 100 miles north, and came home on weekends. He would take the train on Sundays back to Chicago — sometimes we would all see him off at the train station, presumably also his way of arrival on Fridays.

Although no one commented on it, in those days it was surely an unusual way to live, and even then when my sisters and I would start to question why he lived there and she lived here, my mother would simply interpose that that was where his work was and that Auntie Fessner's family had been in Lafayette for decades, owning many farms that had to be overseen, we knew that to be true, by her.

There was one certain fact about her past that we knew. My sisters and I had one time seen a photograph of the 1898 Purdue graduating class; we always knew, without remembering being told, that she had been among the early women Purdue graduates. Now that Thomas was dead and her knees were worse than they had been then, those earlier days when we were children and she still fixed holiday dinners in an alternating manner with my mother, she sat surrounded by piles of books. Mysteriously, those other mysteries about her seemingly dispelled now for me, not by any intentional elucidation by some adult, but more simply by my merging into that world of adults and coming to partially understand it, her books would change in their stacks. Other friends besides my mother, or perhaps the library itself, must have arranged it, periodically bringing new ones and taking the old ones away.

Sitting in the chair opposite hers, the mate to her own winged-backed chair, I would often feel as I had when I was a child.   Then my feet dangled, and the arms were so stuffed that stretching out my own completely did not make resting them normally even possible; but it was the high back that seemed the most disproportionate; it felt just so much higher than my head that sometimes I could, in sitting, easily imagine being sucked into the crack between the seat and back.

In the old-fashioned window seat there were two windows angled sideways from the front one which bulged onto the porch, all hung with real lace curtains — creamy cloth snowflakes, strung together, seat to ceiling — there, I had, one day sometime before she started kindergarten, taught Colleen to read. I had been reading to her, trying hard to make her catch on and somehow after numerous tries of my reading this and that sentence, followed by her repeating each, she suddenly read one sentence and then the one that followed and more.

From those first days when I must have been six years old, on through childhood I had loved going to Auntie Fessner's: Thanksgivings, Christmases, Easters, to sit at the huge oak dining room table; it had to be the darkest in the world with legs each large enough to be a pedestal of its own, the whole thing too huge for its room.

Thomas would be there at the head, the napkins, big as

our laps and the great lace cloth hanging over all of our knees. We listened to the dinner conversation, my sisters and I, waiting for our dinner favorite, whatever the season: Auntie Fessner's homemade raspberry sherbet. She always served it in swan-shaped glass dishes used only for the sherbet. When dinner was over, national and international politics, university politics too, New Yorker articles and cartoons, all discussed, someone would always prevail upon her to recite *The Owl and the Pussycat*: the very long sing-song tale of wonder and woe of love between the owl and the pussycat. They went to sea in a pea-green boat, to the land of milk and honey, all by the light of the moon. We learned it by heart from listening to her. Auntie Fessner would protest with her wonderful laugh, always, while we all fell silent, the adults as quiet as the children, and then she would begin to recite it, all 50-odd verses.

After we had buried Colleen, she said to me one day, as I sat staring in my chair, she in hers, "Layne, your life must go on, you can't change what has happened. You will get over it."

Somehow it seemed I never forgave her for it; I think I may have started to cry when she said it. I never again played her piano in her sitting room, the corner I loved so much, a few ferns over from my chair: the keys of it were as smooth and as heavy as marble, and I never told her of my hardness of heart.

I never told my mother I didn't want to visit anymore. I knew that Auntie Fessner had said it for my own good to try and help me through; I told myself that it didn't matter. I knew that I still loved her. Later I even tried to understand my own recalcitrance, but I know that I never forgave her in my heart, even though I tried and even when she died.

5

THE DRAFT

In April of that year, 1967, Bryan's draft notice came, forwarded from his mother's in Ft. Wayne, Indiana. He had expected it more than I. We were sitting on the Green Door couch: I had received draft notices myself, because of a lack of clarity about the gender of my name, but this one carried import. Bryan, more prepared than I, was quiet.

It was possible then for college students to get draft deferments: one could go to graduate school or medical school, and never have to think about Vietnam. Bryan had already been accepted, surprisingly, into the Indiana University Medical School; his last year's grades had been less than exemplary, and he told the Dean at his interview that he had rather lost interest. They had accepted him anyway; then he had declined their acceptance, all of this months before.

Now Bryan went downtown and signed up to take the exams for pilot training in the Air Force. He started taking flying lessons at the local airport, and he went back for another set of exams. He passed, and the government began a security check. Because he had been in some Eastern European countries two summers earlier, the security check was more thorough; friends called saying the FBI was asking questions about him. Then he was accepted into pilot training. He was to go to a training base for some period of months, longer than a year; but first, there was Officers' Candidate School in July, something I had never heard of, starting after graduation from Purdue in June. Spouses weren't allowed to live there, so I would move like other wives, to whatever pilot training base he was assigned to, in October, assuming he made it through.

During that summer of 1967 while Bryan was in San Antonio, Texas, at Officers' Candidate School, his big brother in the Sigma Chi fraternity was killed in a mountain climbing expedition up Mt. McKinley in Alaska. I heard it in my hometown and Bryan heard it on national news. Mike Gaynor had been one of a party of seven college-aged climbers on the expedition. Trapped by a sudden summer blizzard, four of them were killed.

I went to San Antonio where they let Bryan out of school for a Saturday. Sitting in a rented car in the parking lot with the last few minutes of his mandatory return to base running out, Bryan spoke as he rarely did, outright, blaming himself for Mike's death. Recalling a conversation with Mike about climbing, Bryan's own enthusiasm for it had been the reason that Mike had taken up climbing himself; Bryan said he was certain of it. He could remember the conversation verbatim.

Coincidentally for Bryan and me, I had known Mike all throughout junior high and high school: we went to the same high school, the only only one in West Lafayette; like other towns of large midwestern universities, namely the Big Ten schools, West Lafayette, with the the exception of a village of bookstores at its center, formed a small perimeter around an enormous campus. The thousands of undergraduates were anonymous to us growing up there, but in town, everyone knew everyone. And I knew Bryan's fraternity big brother from years of youth fellowship meetings at the Methodist Church, abutting the village center bookstores - a few blocks from the Sigma Chi house. The three of us made great sense.

Later Mike told me stories about Bryan; there were the amazing times that Bryan would hide up under the eaves of the fraternity, reading the Encyclopedia Britannica while everyone else was cramming for exams from their texts and notes, and then, according to Mike, Bryan would emerge from his hole, come down out of the house and go into the exam where he would inevitably Ace It, whatever it was, usually getting the highest grade of anyone in the house. He made it look easy. His grandmother had given him his Britannicas when he was nine and he had been reading them ever since. More of the Sigma Chi legend about him.

And it was Mike, Bryan told me, who made it possible for him to disappear as he did into the eaves by never telling of his hiding place. Bryan kept the hole through which he climbed upon under the roof, well covered; in fact, only he was small enough to get through it, with Mike hauling him out only when it was necessary during pledging.

Now, in my town of West Lafayette, any self-appoint-ed city historian, the high school principal himself, could tell you of the many young people from West Side who have died in bizarre accidents, both at home and abroad. In the decade of Colleen McCormick, indeed those now famous 1960s, the vice-president of Purdue, one dean, an Eli Lily man, and two ministers, all suffered the untimely deaths of their children, all sons except for Colleen. Everyone in town knows about it. But it is all in the past now because it happened a long time ago. There's a plac-ard even, in the principal's office, placed in honor of all the young athletes killed later in the 1970s and 1980s. That's in the past now, too, they'll say, all those historians. But I wouldn't believe it.

And there's good reason to believe that all those deaths of those young people don't fall so fast into the past.

I'll tell you why. The imprint is still there. But you have to talk to the first-hand recipients, not those who received second hand reports, passed down those decades by way of West Side gossip. You have to take a look in from the skull top to see it on the brain: both brand and branding iron in a heap of embers.

I think the brain of another of my friend's finally burned out from his imprint. He was Cris Gaynor, the brother of Mike Gaynor. We were all in Methodist Youth Fellowship those years together. On that expedition up Mt. McKinley, Mike was one of three Indiana climbers who did-n't make it back, and when Cris, whom I just mentioned, committed suicide some years later in the 1970s, no one could figure it out: he had a bunch of things to be grateful for, they said.

He had a place in the country, a great wife and three wonderful kids, and a Ph.D. in chemistry, but no one men-tioned Mike. I did myself, tell his parents, one time at a concert when I happened to be home for a week-end and saw them for the first time in a long time, that I thought it had more to do with Mike than anything that had happened to him in the 1970s — he had idolized his own older broth-er even in high school — although I had to say I hadn't seen Cris any more recently that I had seen Mike, since just after college. But I think Cris' brain just burned him out, those Jack O'lantern-like ashes, the memory of it. To put it more accurately — the process of trying to make a memory of it. The effort it took to turn his brother into a memory: a Jack O'lantern caved in on itself from the candle-heat.

6

PILOT TRAINING

In the fall, we moved to Moody Air Force Base in Valdosta, Georgia, one of eight Air Force pilot training bases. We arrived in October at what seemed a no man's land of reedy marshes. Spanish moss, hung gray-green on the vegetation, shrubbery and trees alike, forming aisles along the highways. One had to look closely for perceptible evidence of seasons changing. Newly arrived and not yet accommodated to the environs, but noting a lack of color in the leaves, we commented that here in Georgia you would never know that it was fall. I had never been on an Air Force base, so one surprise was followed by another. The security police at the front gate took Bryan's identification papers and orders, then left us in, and we drove in the direction of airplanes and hangers — visible in the distance. Up close, on what seemed at least the size of a large football field there was an enormous collection of small jet airplanes, lined up in symmetrical rows, wingtip to wingtip. The maneuvering for just that accomplishment was something to consider: these were the jet trainers that Bryan had been envying in photos for years. Viewing it, he was not disappointed in his anticipation.

Of the two, the T-37s and the T-38s, training would come first in the T-37s; too many to count were lined up on the front portion of the field, silver in color and more squared-off in appearance than the white and sleek-looking T-38s in rows behind. Beyond both were miles of deserted marshes, a place to practice flying, selected clearly not without some forethought. Within some months Bryan would — running on empty — nearly get lost out near Quitman, a small town some numbers of marshlands west of Valdosta. Thirty-three percent of the class would not make it through pilot training, and, we would hear more of it, the death toll in pilot training was high.

Having seen the jet trainers, we drove the twelve miles into town, where we rented a house the same afternoon. Training was to last about eighteen months: three segments, I learned, that were to consist of training, first in a

Cessna at a civilian airport outside of town for four months; then another six months in the T-37; and finally, six months in a T-38. They were the jets we had seen on the field when we first drove onto the base. Both T-37s and T-38s are fitted with two seats: sided by side for instructor and student pilot in the T-37; front and back, in the T-38, for student and instructor pilots, respectively, with the exception of instrument flying training in which the instructor pilot occupies the front seat and the student pilot occupies the rear seat, flying under a canvas hood with no visual reference outside of the aircraft. The respective pilots are referred to as front-seaters and back-seaters: in training the front seat is for the instructor pilot and the back is for the student. Upon the student pilot's attaining a certain level of proficiency, the two reverse positions: student pilot in front, and instructor in back.

The beginning of the year's training did not seem unusual, listening to talk of Cessna flying. But soon, moving to the T-37 and then the T-38, learning take-offs and landings gave way to aerobatics, formation flying, and finally to flying "under the bag" as they all called it, instrument flying. Bryan made it all sound simple. It didn't surprise me that he studied little, and it seemed no different from his days at Purdue. Transitions from the Cessna to the T-37 and from the T-37 to the T-38 each required passing what were termed check-rides, but I rarely knew when he had either a written or a flying exam. I knew the wash-out rate, a phrase to become very familiar for flunking out of training, was very high. Over one-third of the class had failed by the mid-point of the training year. But not until years later did I learn Bryan had had trouble during T-37 training. It had to do with an instructor pilot, named Marsh, and the last T-37 check-ride.

I remembered that Bryan had taken an extra check-ride. It didn't seem unusual then. We had both overslept, and being late, Bryan had for once seemed nervous. Leaving in a rush that morning, he told me Marsh, his instructor pilot was giving him a hard time. That was the first I knew of trouble in T-37 training.

Ten years later at least, one time when we were driving to Ft. Wayne to visit Bryan's mother, he finished the story about this instructor pilot. In a gas station while he was filling the tank and I was leaning out the window, he ended the story about the last checkride. He told me Marsh had stated to him, prior to the checkride, that he had no intention of passing Bryan.

"Can you believe, he actually got up on the table, and walked on my checklist? He made footprints on it." Bryan started to laugh derisively. I looked at him blankly while feeling appalled. We were driving out of the gas station now. "No, that's pretty hard to believe." I really wondered if Bryan were making it up, just to get me going, never mind the missing years. I stayed calm and looked straight ahead.

"How come he did it?" I tried to sound casual, wishing he had told me about it when it had happened. "Did you figure that out?"

"I guess he was making his point. He told me again that he had no intention of passing me."

"So, what happened?" I asked.

"Well, it just so happened," Bryan was going to finally finish the story now. "That there was a classroom of guys across the hall. The door was open, and they had been watching it all. When Marsh got up on the table, I told him what he could do with my checklist, and the guys cracked up."

"So, then?" I asked.

"He passed me."

That same summer we took what turned into a memorable trip to the Everglades. Getting to the state line from Valdosta required little time. Driving, we learned that Valdosta was was the last town on the interstate running though Georgia into Florida; the remainder of the drive to the Everglades themselves, however, took another six hours, with our stopping at two alligator farms in route. This was a way of getting into the swing of things, according to Bryan. He would really like to have taken the time, he said, to try some alligator wrestling. Nevertheless, it was 5:00 already and we hadn't started into the Everglades.

Route 70, going east and west through the Everglades, called Alligator Alley, by the local inhabitants, was seemingly totally deserted at this time of day of traffic on the road, and devoid as well, of gas stations along it. Supposedly we were looking for alligators in the wild along the road too, but it occurred to me that Bryan was driving so fast that sighting an alligator would be difficult.

"Why don't you slow down," I said on the pretense of

wanting to look. In those days, the Shelby Mustang was a new car. I looked over; the speedometer said 120 miles per hour.

"If you don't slow down," I went on in a few moments, "You will have to have to let me out. This is too fast for me."

This time it was clear. He had to be ignoring me.

"OK that's it. I want out." The car slowed and stopped. Apparently he had been listening to me. Now, looking straight ahead, he was waiting to see if I would really do it.

I opened the door. Too late, I thought, to back down now. I closed it carefully without slamming it.   And off Bryan went in a roar.

I started walking, not looking much at either roadside, wondering how long it would be before darkness had set in altogether.   I didn't have long to consider it as minutes later, a trucker pulled to a halt. A man and a woman together in the cab of a semi-trailer. I took my chances and climbed up and in, thanking them for the ride. We rode, making some polite conversation about the weather this evening as though this were a perfectly ordinary place to be hitch-hiking. A few miles down the road I heard, before I saw, Bryan, roaring back up the road.

Trying not to be visible to him, without being so obvious as cause the truck driver and his wife wonder about me, I scooted down in my corner of the semi-seat. Bryan would have a hard time seeing me up this high even if I weren't slouching down, nor could I actually see him, just the top of the car. A few minutes later, I saw it go by again. Driving faster yet, he was getting apprehensive I was sure, about what had happened to me. I enjoyed the idea that he would have to be wondering if I had been sucked into the Everglades by an alligator. Surprisingly, a small town appeared. I suggested this would be a fine place to drop me off.

The truck driver pulled up at a small diner, I thanked them both and got out to walk into the diner as though this had been my destination all along.

Inside, I ordered a hamburger and a coke; five minute later Bryan showed up. He sat down, taking a look at what I was eating and ordered the same, a hamburger and coke for himself. We made small conversation about both the diner and dinner without mentioning our separate means of arrival; then we got back into the car to head on across the last half of Alligator Alley.

7

VIETNAM IN AN F-4

Never having lived in California, I was looking forward to a move there, but I didn't much want to hear about it from everyone else. Does anyone. We get sick of hearing, talking California, seeing it on TV, those of us who are from elsewhere. But there are things that have nothing to do with anything you hear about it - promises, promises - they are little known facts, and interesting ones, at that, about its geography: two in particular. One - has to do with the shape of the sky at night. It is very high and has a curved aspect.

It is different from that in midwestern and eastern cities and is apparent when the land is flat and open. It simply looks dome-like. I myself have seen it around those deserted Air Force bases both north and south: test pilot and F-4 fighter bases south on the Mojave Desert or the SR-71 base up north: star-lines you can follow up the dome in those wide open weed-spaces. As I mentioned, there is a difference between the midwestern and eastern cities' skies. In the Eastern cities the night comes down between the buildings to fill up the spaces. I am thinking that in Ft. Wayne, Indiana, Bryan's home town there is one particular street corner where I always noted the darkness of sky at night. It was a block between his mother's house and Nick's Rib Bar, a place where we invariably ate when we were in town, no matter how short the visit. Poured down from somewhere - that black running. Maybe you could feel india ink taking form around you and then turn it all upside down and pour the city back into it.

Two - has to do with the shape of the land; my thought is that the ancient mariners may have had something in the idea that the earth is flat; not only that, but if the whole U.S. lays flat and solid to the California line, where the Sierra stands its border up and down, from there on California floats on the ocean which, in turn, must creep in under its coast. I think the high dry weeds and sage brush blow harder in the wind up north of Sacramento where they fly the SR-71, because of these land undulations, and I swear, there is a low rippling of the roads themselves, as they curve into the foothills and on up into the Sierra. I think I have felt it - whether in the hot Shelby Cobra or the fat Ford station wagon.

The drop-off of the flat earth, needless to say, is the western California coast. There is a promontory just south of San Francisco on Route 10l; hardly anyone drives it, strangely enough. I think you can see — I know — promises, promises, the edge of the earth there: dazed daisies are glued down to the bluffs and because of the vertigo I need always to go inland from there.

During the time that Bryan went through F-4 training on the Mojave Desert we literally lived on the desert. Or at least, we almost literally lived on the desert. The base, George Air Force Base, was — still is — located close to Victorville, California, which itself is on the road that runs between Los Angeles and Las Vegas. The two in-between towns or stop-offs on one's way to or from either, are Victorville in California and Barstow in Nevada. Barstow, closest to Las Vegas, seems a long way across the Mojave Desert from Victorville which sits up out of the San Bernadino Valley, some 80 miles above LA. The Cajon Pass — a small pass really — is in between Victorville, which is inland up on the desert, and LA, down on the coast. Victorville is a town of concrete, a sort of oasis, and it is ten miles from George Air Force Base.

That was where you lived as an officer, it was tacitly understood; if you were among the enlisted personnel, you could live in Adelanto instead of Victorville, and it was just three miles from the base. George Air Force Base was flat-out in the middle of the Mojave, and in Adelanto the sand ran through the single street, just as it did around the town when the wind was up: no concrete to hold it down. Before I came with Kelly, Bryan had rented a house there — it actually had a white picket fence around it — and it was close to the base, a mile from the end of the runway from which came a constant stream of Air Force F-4s not many feet overhead.

Kelly had been born in my hometown while Bryan was at a month's radar school in Tucson; he met me, Kelly and our German shepherd Smokey, at the LA airport, and we went to Adelanto.

The only advantage to the place we had, according to parents and friends who in coming to see us inevitably commented first on the disruption from the jets, was that Bryan could come back and forth easily, it was so close; we both liked it for the reason that it was close to the runway and we could watch and hear the F-4s. But we learned not to insist on anyone else's enjoyment of it. The place itself was actually a hole of a house, constructed of cement block, without even an air conditioner for the desert heat. There was an air cooler of some sort that broke down regularly, the plumbing was terrible, and we had to put the washing machine in what was sort of a garage, a place too spidery for the car, more like a barn. There wasn't much in compensation, we came to tacitly understand from friends and relatives, for the awful noise that came with the house in Adelanto.

The garage was chock-full of black widow spiders, that being the reason for not putting the car in it. I figured the black widows wouldn't bother the washer or, if they did, they wouldn't survive the cycles of washing and rinsing, and we didn't have a dryer, so I hung clothes on the line. Naively, the first day there, I put Kelly in a rocker out in the back-yard with me while I was hanging clothes, and my neighbor came over and told me bluntly I'd better straighten up: get some shoes on and get my baby up on the porch, unless I wanted to risk either of us being bitten by scorpions. "Check your shoes, every time you put them on, too," she said.

She went on. "There are coyotes, up in the hills - you can hear them at night. Sometimes you can see them."

"Do they ever come in close?" I asked.

"Yes, but not too often. But you do have to be careful at night. Someone got killed last summer from a coyote attack."

Bryan had been telling me these things: that the woman had told him to be careful about when I came, and to pass on to me, but I had really not listened carefully. The coyotes, I didn't think too much about, nor the black widows which I thought I had under control. But the scorpions — she showed me one in a jar — I became appreciative of: they would be indistinguishable from the sand in color, and they were so spindly in shape that one would certainly have to look twice to observe them.

Bryan's dad came for a visit, and, to our surprise, already having had a good bit of disgruntled company coming during the summer, the place didn't seem to bother him a bit. We ate out at places in Victorville, the George Officers' Club, and the Roy Rogers Ranch, and, nightly after our dinners out, we started making peaches flambe in a chafing dish his dad had bought in Victorville. He stayed long enough for it to become the summer's ritual: we would put Kelly to bed, and then the three of us would enjoy the wait for the sun to set, sitting in make-shift lawn chairs in the front yard with its scrubby desert-dry view, flat to the mountain horizon. Soon we could turn out the lights, light the cognac and watch it burn blue over the peaches. Neither Bryan nor his dad nor I ever mentioned the fall coming up — I knew I should be thinking about a job — just as we hadn't mentioned earlier our crummy house for the summer, its lack of a stove, the washer in the garage, the lack of a dryer, and proper air conditioner: on base, we never discussed the fact that every F-4 there was camouflaged, and that the truth was — Bryan was training for Vietnam. We talked flying as usual, with Bryan filling his dad in on his training up until this point and now: daily bomb runs up in the Owens Valley, 60 degrees to the desert floor; the desert was the best place to be practicing.

More than one or two F-4s had recently stalled into the desert floor. As far as I could tell, it was best not to think of any of it now. We took Kelly to Disneyland regularly. Sometimes at night we'd drive in to LA, picking different places to go and see. Friday nights we started going the 80 miles down the Cajon pass into San Bernardino and the outskirts of LA to the various drive-in movies we could find with Kelly in a slingbed and Smokey, our now full-grown German shepherd beneath it, in the back seat of our hot-rod Shelby Cobra. We were going to the movies.

At the end of the summer, I found a roommate for the upcoming year. Her husband, also in F-4 training this summer, would be in Da Nang for the year. All summer long, we had been going down the pass ourselves in the daytimes once a week into LA to shop at a different mall every time. This time, we climbed into her big station wagon taking Kelly with us to job hunt.

We headed first for the City of Hope Medical Center which ran regular ads in the LA Sunday Times for laboratory technicians, and then the next time, we made the rounds of some of the school teaching districts for Susan to find a job. In the end, I took a job in Indianapolis in the laboratory of my former advisor at Indiana University who was to be on sabbatical in Israel for the year. He needed someone to oversee the mouse work of a leukemia grant.

Susan then found a teaching job in Indianapolis, and we rented a big old house which had room for us all, including Kelly, not a year old, Smokey, Susan's two Afghan hounds, and her five cats, having decided that with our menageries, even separately, we would probably do better for the year if we tried to find a place to live together.

It worked. The house that we rented was on the block next to the block of the Indiana governor's mansion: bought by a Mr. Haverford who owned an elevator company. He didn't want his own home, in this block, to become part of an integrated neighborhood. So, having bought every house on the block, he rented them to whomever he chose; he didn't care about all of our animals, only that we were in the house. We had to not care about his ulterior motives because it was the only house that we could find whose owner would rent to us. In its day, it had been elegant: three-storied and fronted with a large leaded-glass window in front entry.

We had just driven across country and this was apparently it - the beginning of a year, literally on opposites sides of the earth for all of us. Both Bryan and Ralph would be flying F-4 aerial reconnaissance over Vietnam: Bryan from Ubon; and Ralph, from Da Nang on the Vietnam coast. I hadn't yet located Ubon, Thailand, on any map. Bryan was sorting through his guns in the bedroom that was going to be mine, making ready to clean the pile of them and prepare them for a year's storage.

The room was suffocatingly hot; all four of us, were trying to make sure the furnace was working, so we had it running in the September heat. It was 85 degrees - Indian Summer was familiar to Bryan and me, but not to Susan and Ralph who were complaining of it. I was occupied with what I thought was the superfluousness of Bryan's developing gun routine ritual. I knew Susan and Ralph were discussing the upcoming year apart, making plans for an R & R in Hawaii. Overhearing them, I thought that Bryan and I should try to talk about it, the length of it was to be real, too. But departing from the Indianapolis Airport for Thailand, neither of us had, or seemingly could, mention the year coming, to one another.

The most reliable fighter-bomber of the Air Force Tactical Air Command is the F-4, commonly called the F-4 Phantom; according to it pilots, the F-4 is the most utilitarian of the Air Force fighter-bombers. Vietnam models were the F-4C, F-4D, and F-4Es and collectively the F-4s could be flown as fighter-bombers, as escort aircraft for other fighters, and in aerial reconnaissance for selecting bombing targets for other aircraft or for assessing the damage following bombing by these aircraft.

The F-4s were stationed in Vietnam at Da Nang Army Base and in Thailand at various bases which went unmentioned in the U.S., even by the press, the reason being that Thailand, separated from Vietnam only by Laos, was nonetheless officially neutral in the Vietnam War. Somehow the U.S. Government managed to preclude press coverage of these bases. As a result, they were virtually unknown to the U.S. Public as well.

As it was, there were five bases of the Royal Thai Air Force that were used by the U.S, one of which was also used by the U.S. CIA; on a map the five appear as symmetrically arranged as color splotches on a painter's palette, each seemingly equidistant from the edge of the slightly distorted sphere that represents Thailand on a map.

Likewise, all Thai Air Force Bases are also approximately equal distances from one another. Starting at the top and middle northernmost border, where Burma to the left and Laos to the right merge in a common border over Thailand, if one follows the circumference of the circle in either direction, there are five evenly spaced sites of Air Bases within its border.

Along the right map edge of Thailand, Laos leans down, toward Thailand, something like a profile of ET: squat head and body bulging top and bottom, a long snake-like neck in the middle equaling the Eastern border of Thailand with the ET-type head bent, facing Thailand. Vietnam itself lies one more inch to the map's right on the deformed ET-like back of Laos, skinnier in its middle and bulging at its top, resembling some strange lily-like flower.

Within Thailand, on the right map-border, Nakhan Phanom is located one-o'clock, to the north and east, closest to the Laotian border; Ubon straight south of NKP, as Nakhan Phanom is called, is at five-o'clock to the Laotian border; Utapao sits at the bottom and middle of Thailand; then come Korat and Udorn along the left map-border adjacent to Burma, mirror images to Nakhan Phanom and Ubon, by a fold of the country in half over itself. Utapao at the bottom is the only base without a match on the opposite side of the country to make a pair, a single eye on the war focused up through the Laotian-shaped ET and back on down into the lily-like Vietnam. That's where the planes plunged from into the jungles of Vietnam.

These bases were jumbled with C141 transports, F104s, F-4 fighter-bombers, B-52s, the EB66 radar planes, Laotian T-28s. Line them up on the Thai runways, dump them down the Laotian hollowed eye, and look up close for the Ho Chi Minh Trail.

According to Walter Cronkite, Udorn was the control point of the Indochina War. It was also the center of the CIA intelligence activities and a huge supply base as well: Laotian T-28s came there for their refurbishments. NKP, plied with electronic sensors and a storage center for TV-guided or laser-guided bombs, was said to be wired like a pin-ball machine every night. It was the heart of the electronics war on the Ho Chi Minh Trail. Utapao was a B-52 base. F-104s and EB66s were stationed at Korat. The F-4s were stationed at Udorn and at Ubon.

Bryan was to be stationed at Ubon, Thailand, and from there he would aerial reconnaissance over Vietnam as an F-4 Forward Air Controller, known as an F-4 FAC. The group he came to fly with out of Ubon called themselves the Wolf-FACS.

During both his time of F-4 training on the Mojave Desert, a year's F-4 flying in Vietnam, August to August, 1969 to 1970, there were many more facts that I should have known about the war. Bryan said next-to-nothing about it. Later, after he had been back for some months, he gave me his most vivid description of that time: a flight toward the mouth of some cave in South Vietnam, upside-down and 50 feet off the ground, and the cave's opening had been flown for fun. The rest of the year's flying was altogether a smooth-over by him. What I did know came most clearly in the dark of a night driving down the Owens Valley which is on Route 199 in the center of the state of

California. The route parallels the Pacific and the Sierra, but is in between and is closest to the Sierra-Range side of the state.

Commenting that we were passing China Lake to the left where they were starting to practice bomb runs, Bryan slowed and I leaned in his direction to my left to look. It was too dark to see. I knew that, in fact, the lake was dried to the bottom with no water in it. Just the mid-summer week prior, his F-4 training had progressed to bombing practice.

It was a period of time that Bryan talked rather extensively of the flying. "If you stall out," he had said, "You're dead."

His dad, a retired Army colonel, commented that he knew the danger, dropping his head slowly downward and propping the fingertips of each hand against those of the other, tent-like, apparently thinking concentratedly about bombing practice. His legs were stretched out in front of him in a lawn chair our crummy house behind him and the Mojave Desert straight ahead, and we were about to eat dinner. My heart was pounding. The night a few weeks earlier, driving down through the Owens Valley, I had been thinking hard about making it to Boron, a town that consisted, appropriately enough, of a garish string of gas stations at the end of the barren stretch of road. We were running on empty and had, I said, more miles to go than gas for them. Bryan's comment was that there was enough to ride into town on our fumes.

"So," I said, trying to concentrate back on dinner, "At what angle do you head down for the bombing run?"

"Sixty degrees," he said.

"Isn't that incredibly steep?"

"Sure, you don't want to stall-out on your way out either," Bryan said. "You can't pull out of those stalls. Two guys bought the farm already this week."

I didn't have to ask to know what he meant. Living at the Green Door, Bryan had more than described F-4s to me and had said the only way he would go to Vietnam was in one.

Perhaps now I can say that an F-4 Phantom had then, and probably still has now, an aura unlike any other Air Force jet. Camouflaged completely or silvered and inscribed by the USAF — it was then considered ominous, sometimes described as wicked, in appearance. Stationary on a runway or in a hanger, the F-4 does not lose its aura, and moving in the flame of its own afterburner, it flies in constant thundering on the runways of its landings and take-offs and in the air through which it runs, wings down, if you will: you could not - not watch it. If one did not see the danger for which it was sent out on sortie, even over the California sky of the now-imaginary China Lake, one indeed, had to be wearing blinders.

8

AN INTERIM

In the winter of the first year in Northern California, we skied. Bryan had returned safely from his year's stint in F-4s in Vietnam only to find himself likely to go again, this time in a B-52. Stationed in Northern California for training: Sacramento at Mather Air Force Base, l971, it was an especially cold winter for California. We smiled smugly, coming from the Midwest, at the evening news following a snowstorm that left rifts of snow for the first time in years on Mt. Tamalpais just north of San Francisco.

There was a run on propane torches at hardware stores all over the Bay Area and up in Sacramento as well. Pipes were frozen everywhere; above ground, they were unprotected from the freezing weather. Two days later we were waiting in line for a torch ourselves and learning how to melt the water in frozen pipes: the pipes in our house, just like in everyone else's, were above ground and frozen solid.

Things seemed surprising for quite some time that way. On moving there, coming down out of the Sierra foothills, we decided we would buy a house in the hills and then found that this capitol of California, for reasons the settlers in the Gold Rush days knew better than we, was nearly flat. We bought a house in what had been an olive grove, the hilliest part of Sacramento overlooking the American River and then wondered about getting in and out in the winter when it snowed, forgetting at first that it never snowed in this strip of land between the Sierra mountain range east of us and the Pacific Coast to the west.

Neither of us had ever been on skis, nor had Bill, Bryan's B-52 instructor pilot, older than we, who came to spend as many of his off-work hours with the two of us as he spent with Bryan, teaching him how to fly B-52s. We would rent them from the base recreation center where the sergeant handed them out, gauging the proper lengths for our heights. Just long black generic skis, $2 per day, all seeming much too long as measured by our heights. Being close to six feet tall, the sergeant gave me a pair that were 200 centimeters, over six feet long. He refused to give any of us shorter ones, saying only that we should trust him.

We drove straight up from the base through northern Sacramento, to Interstate 80 at its midway point between San Francisco and Lake Tahoe; then, on up 80 to one of the ski resorts where we would strap on our skis as though we knew what we were doing; we would give one another a last look and push off on our midweek discount ski lift tickets.

Much of the time he was on skis Bill spent laughing. He usually moved around carefully, gliding gingerly down the beginner slopes; he said he hated heights. I asked why he liked to fly, then, and he would insist that flying was totally different, that there was no sensation of height in flying.

Bryan kept asking us both on different trips if we didn't want to go to the top of Soda Springs; the advanced slope ran into an intermediate one, which in turn ran into the beginner's slope, different from Squaw Valley where each grade was a separate slope. Here, all of it was one huge long ski run, steeper and steeper toward the top, with a mild incline at the bottom, ending at the lodge; Bill's answer was standard, giving Bryan what we all thought of as his movie star smile: "You go — a drink sounds good to me. I'll meet you in the bar."

"I think I'll go halfway up in the chair lift," Bryan was persistent this particular time. None of us had yet even learned how to turn. "It doesn't look that hard. Come on and go with me."   He meant either of us.

"No way," was Bill's laugh and answer.

"Don't look at me." I answered before he asked again. He was looking at me now. "I can't even get down the beginners' slope without falling."

The seat was huge, large enough for at least three people, and once in it, I wished Bryan had persuaded Bill to come along. Even keeping one's skis straight ahead in the chairlift as it took off from the platform was an effort. At the intermediate chairlift platform already the height was intimidating.

"Don't you want to go to the top?" I heard him saying it, and I knew that he wasn't looking at me.

"Don't be ridiculous." The platform came and went,

and it was too late now. The slope steepened; breathing in and out, I felt the clouds close. I was getting nervous. I thought of how I hated heights as much as Bill.

This platform was different from the one lower down, a longer jump onto it, and no one appeared to be there to grab you as you slipped off the lift. Already it was almost too late again. Bryan plopped himself onto the ground, falling because it was too high for him to land on his feet. I followed suit. Getting up I found a member of the ski patrol watching me: the same one who had helped me up from the J-bar on the beginner slope. I had fallen off it earlier in the day and he had stopped the J-bar altogether, the expression on his face just confirming the ridiculousness of my even being atop this advanced slope.

Bryan was at the edge, looking down. We talked about how to maneuver down. I knew that the clouds were some distance up, but the skiers at the bottom were, in fact, quite small in appearance. We were actually up some hundreds of feet. The surface at the top seemed to angle up slightly before the precipitous drop. We concurred that getting down properly, criss-crossing and turning back at each side, was beyond us since we did not know how to turn.

"I'm going," he said, "Just straight down."

"The whole way?"

"Well, I guess so." He looked over the edge, leaning forward again. I eased myself closer to take a look too. "If you don't want to do it, I'll tell the ski patrol guy to come on back up and they can stop the chair lift for you to get in and ride down." He was looking uneasy. "I think the seat is low enough. You'll be able to get up into it." He was smiling. We both knew with my longer legs I would have a better chance for that than he.

"O.K., but first maybe I can figure it out." I went on, "Let me see how you do." My sitting down theory seemed irrelevant. I would be going far too fast.

He headed straight down; in a minute or two he was off the advanced slope and onto the intermediate slope. Midway, becoming diminutive to my view, he fell, then got up apparently unhurt and skied the rest of the way without mishap.

I eased myself over and and started sliding straight down. Later I didn't remember falling, wherever I did it, somewhere there along the intermediate slope, and I was more than glad to get to the bottom. Bryan and I began to laugh now that we were safe, commenting only that at the top it was steeper than it looked from the bottom. Bill took a look at us and apparently decided to go along with our preposterousness, making little comment also, and we all climbed into the car, struggling with our oversized skis, assigned as usual, by the sergeant, and discussed as we started home, where we would stop along the way for some mulled wine.

Weekends the three of us, taking Kelly with us, roamed San Francisco. We made the rounds of bizarre stores that we read about; often they were no longer in existence when we located their addresses.

At a costume store one day, Bill nearly taunted Bryan into buying a pink gorilla suit, $800. We had been in a neighboring gun store, where Bill and I had managed to persuade Bryan to wait before buying an anniversary issue of a Colt 45 revolver. Passing the costume store, we all headed in the door in unison. The gorilla suits, one of which was on display in the window, were hung on a rack of sorts in the store's mezzanine. The downstairs portion of the store was almost a perfect square in shape, and racks of costumes and accoutrements made passage around the downstairs circuitous: in the middle portion of the downstairs, an old-fashioned wide flight of steps led up from the confusion of costumiery to the balcony that circled three of the four walls. Bill and I had come inside to humor Bryan, that we all knew. Poking through the racks, we heard a voice that was Bryan's, "Hey, guys, take a look." He was leaning over the mezzanine railing with the top of the pink gorilla suit on. Shreds of pink fur fell over the railing, and the gorilla suit shoulders, twice the size of Bryan's own, made him appear bulbously squat but enormous.

Bill's comment, "You look great," was followed by his goading Bryan to buy it. "The tag says it's only $800. Maybe you could fly in it." Bryan disappeared behind the railing and was gone, and we saw him next outside the building, peering through the window, as though in surprise at our presence in the store.

Another day, we found a herpetarium in a residential neighborhood by the beach. It was a large square room behind pale yellow clapboard walls. It had been converted from a ground floor apartment and symmetrically took up one street corner with a single small door on one side, which we learned was locked electronically from the inside. Its windows were totally obscured with venetian blinds, and a small sign stated that children under twelve were not allowed inside. Within, each of us taking a turn staying with Kelly outside the door, Bryan made ready to buy a tarantula and then a boa constrictor. Following our suggestion of a California king snake that Bryan said would not be satisfactory, we somehow persuaded him to wait altogether until another time: his design had been to take them home as pets by holding Kelly on our three laps in the front seat, putting black widow and boa constrictor, boxed, in the back seat for the ride back to Sacramento.

Other odd places in San Francisco that we read about, we became accustomed to finding closed, changed into something else: subsumed silently into the city; another store, an office, an apartment, something. We sat Kelly up on the wide window seat at the Cliff House on the ocean and we watched the seals on the rocks and drank coffee with Irish whiskey and cream while we talked of what and where we would eat those nights and of the places we did or didn't find that particular day.

We talked about renting an apartment in San Francisco. Then we could stay whole weekends, picnic in Golden Gate Park often and go to the Planetarium afterwards and go to more organ concerts, Sundays, at the Palace of the Legion of Honor.

We would buy another motorcycle so we could all ride the city streets the way Bryan and I had the first weekends we traveled to San Francisco. We had been all over and through the city on it; in and out of Chinatown, squeaking by the cars on the narrow streets, up on Telegraph Hill, up on Twin Peaks, down across the sand-splattered road by the beach to Lake Merced. Now we had to do it in twos, while the third waited at the end of the ride. With two motorcycles, the three of us could ride at once.

Then we could rent a glider from the glider port up the interstate toward Lake Tahoe or better yet, buy one and a carrier for it, and buy as well, a sailboat to sail from Tiburon into the San Francisco Bay. Bill wanted to do those two things the most.

And following World War II, they said, someone flew a fighter, in celebration of the War's end, underneath the

Golden Gate, so the two of them - Bryan and Bill - would make preparation for one day flying their B-52 under the Golden Gate, if it would fit.

9

THE AFORETHOUGHT

Squares of coloured glass falling through my life again, in a kaleidoscope of glass. They show us all in a swirl of snapshots: our families and friends in a time paralleling and colliding with the war: F-4 training in Southern California, Vietnam for twelve months, B-52 training in Northern California, Vietnam another nine months, and finally after it all when the seams, so to speak, of our lives, more than just yours and mine I think, gave way thinly and disintegrated, I'm tempted to say into smithereens.

Back in Monterey, one weekend between F-4 and B-52 tours and training in Southern and Northern California — it was still a time of some innocence on military matters — I am haunted by a single snapshot of myself, more than any other of my life. I see the sun, low over the mountains, myself staring at a rainbow, watching it run its thin-lined watercolors down the edges into the haze. A pink stucco building still stands at the end of the Monterey pier, countless sets of tic-tac-toe windows trimmed in white. It is a scene for which I need to know the reason of my remembering. Is it a question of pain? An organ grinder's monkey, tiny and donned in a sunny checked suit, covered with red and blue hearts, grasps my small daughter's hand, then cranks the handle of the gold-gilt organ. Music falls through the haze: pink and white chalkdust to breathe and taste. I can still feel the tumult in my chest, bending over both, smiling so easily seemingly, my own real heart pounding in undisclosed unease. The organ grinder holds his hat for change, and the answer, I think, is yes, it is a question of pain. For us all. I look and remember the feel of the silky minidress that I wore and of my hair, heavy and pinned at my neck. Why, when I remember it all so differently, do I look so perfect in that print of years ago? Perhaps to fool me later, to fool me, say, now?

10

VIETNAM IN A B-52

The intercom communications during the bomb run and just before and after made an interesting contrast with the first few missions. When we first went to Hanoi, getting a SAM shot at you was enough to raise everyone's voice a few octaves, and often you would hear the EW blurt out something like:"PILOT! SAMTWELVEO'CLOCK-THREERINGSCOMINGTHIS WAY!!!" On the night of the 26th, I remember a call that went something like this; "Uh...Pilot, SAM...five o'clock, three and a half rings...uh...no biggie, press on." And on the bomb run, if you didn't know better, (by looking outside) you would have sworn you were on a normal training mission back in the states. The guys were cool personified as they commented, (looking at the radar scope) "Yeah, there's the target..there's the offsets..O.K., no sweat." As we came off the target, the sky to the northeast lit up with a tremendous flare, as a B-52 blew up in the air.

> **Major Bill Stocker**
> **December 26, l972**
> **B-52 Bomber in Action**
> **Squadron Signal Publications, Inc.**

A MITO was what they called it: a special B-52 training event in which minimum time interval take-offs were designed to get the B-52 alert force aircraft air borne before incoming missiles strike the airfield. Bill and Bryan had asked if I wanted to watch, so I was situated on a small grass mound, holding Kelly, above the runway ready for their take-off. Three B-52s were to take off with fifteen second spacings on the runway between them. There would be turbulence from the jet engines and wake turbulence from the aircraft wings to make it dangerous for the number two and number three aircraft. But the three took off in what seemed to be briefer than fifteen second time intervals, two looked almost simultaneous, lumbering down the runway and lifting heavily into the visible plane over the runway, then disappearing into the northern California sky.

I planned to come back to this spot, the best to see from, and watch them land in the afternoon. I did errands and headed home. Opening the door, I found them sitting in the living room feet up on the coffee table, both of them still wearing sunglasses and dressed in flight suits and boots. Deciding they were waiting for me to appear and ask what had happened, I didn't comment.

The two of them were talking about going to the Auburn art fair as though they had traveled the 90 miles up into the Sierra by car. I gave in to my curiosity. "So what were you doing at the Auburn art fair?" Auburn, in the Sierra foothills east of Sacramento, wasn't any wider, even corner to corner, than the base runway was long. There was no way to land it.

"Didn't we tell you?" Bill said, "We had two engine flame-outs on take-off."

"I don't remember your saying that, no."

"We thought you would be able to tell it, " said Bryan, "Didn't the take- off look funny? We wondered if you could see the smoke, but maybe you were too far away." It was true, the take-off had looked odd. One of the B-52s, so huge even from a distance, after making it into the air just off the ground, had veered severely to the left before becoming air-borne.

"I saw one of them go off sideways," I said, "But I thought perhaps it was part of the take-off formation of the three planes."

"Hardly," said Bryan. He wasn't just being diffident. Rather, it was apparent that he was somewhat unnerved thinking about it again.

"I told Bill to take it, but he told me just to hang in there."

"He did just great." Bill was matter of fact. I learned that the double flame out was probably caused, or at least aggravated, by disruption of the inlet air to the jet engines caused by the turbulence from the preceding aircraft. Bryan and Bill had, so to speak, been to the Auburn art fair because all of the local FAA controllers and West Coast Strategic Air Command were on the radar and radios, watching and advising the B-52 as to routing for burning off fuel during the next hours before landing. The fire hazard in landing was too too great to land with a full load. So, while being vectored past Auburn, the FAA controller had asked if they could see the Art Fair going on that day.

The special attention to this B-52 was based upon recent experience: no one in the West Coast Command wanted a crash like East Coast SAC had had in Miami the week before when a B-52 had gone down in a residential neighborhood.

B-52 training was split between two bases: Mather Air Force Base in Sacramento, and Merced Air Force Base, about 100 miles south of Sacramento in the San Joaquin Valley. Bill was stationed at Mather Air Force Base as an instructor pilot at first and later, as the squadron commander.

In the beginning, when we first lived in Sacramento however, Bryan was doing a commuting of sorts to Merced for three months' B-52 training. After finishing training at Merced Air Force Base and going through another six months' training at Mather, it became evident that he would be going to Vietnam again. This was to be in July, 1972. Bryan had said that the deal with a B-52 assignment was that, having gone to Vietnam in an F-4, there would be no circumstances under which he would have to go again.

Things weren't working out that way. We, or at least I, hadn't realized, until the word came, that it would become fact. He upgraded from co-pilot to pilot within a couple of months, so he would be going as an aircraft commander with a total crew of six members.

Toward the end of the training, just prior to being sent, he was assigned his own crew. As a Mather crew, they would be stationed on Guam, one of two B-52 bases used for flying over Vietnam. I had heard him talk of a Major John Dearborn, the electronics warfare officer with whom he had been flying regularly in the recent months and who, he said, had taught him a great deal about the workings of a B-52. Major Dearborn was thirty-seven, almost ten years older than Bryan, one of two black crew airmen, we later learned, and a man of extensive flying experience and expertise. Lieutenant Clark, like Bryan, was younger and less-experienced. He was twenty-seven, a year younger than Bryan and in his first year from navigator training. Also like Bryan, his desire to fly had been lifelong. The other three members of the crew I met for the first time the day we all went to Merced to see them off for Guam.

The day before their departure the crew flew their B-52 to Merced, where we all met them the next day. Bryan's mother and grandmother had come from Indiana for good-byes; that day I drove the 30-odd miles from our house on the south side of Sacramento to Merced Air Force Base: down the hill, across the American River on the track of asphalt unlacing itself out of town, dust-grey at the Sunrise Mall above our house, gleaming black in the bare-field heat where it hooks up to Route 99, below the city.

The route was ploughed through the San Joaquin Valley, trucked to death — no wonder a town named Truckee? — it is the main north-south California route for the transport of agricultural products: open-bed semi-trailers move through the valley from spring, which starts in February in California, through the hot fall, and the fruits and vegetables follow the changes of season. The highway is littered with samplings and it is replete with oil slick after tangential oil slick, one of which on the end of my journey to Merced, had landed Bryan on his Honda 750 the night prior to my last birthday, smack in the middle of the rice fields as he was leaving the base. It was a night he had come to surprise me, sneaking out of the BOQ like out of a dorm, to come home for my birthday.

That night of my birthday, Brian had appeared at 7 AM, after laying his bike down, as he put it to me, on one of those oil slicks, this one on the freeway on-ramp right off base. He was getting onto Route 99 in Merced to head north up the valley.

"My bike's in bad shape." He smiled while saying it .

"So, how come you are OK?"

"Well, I probably have a couple of cracked ribs." He smiled again, the same old something leering in it, defiance to the world, and to me, too. I had known it since I had known him. Unusual undertakings, either physical or mental, he took uniquely as challenges to be mastered, and the harder, the better. "I wasn't sure I could get it up off the ground — the front wheel is really bent-up, and the engine sounds bad. Anyway, Happy Birthday."

"Thanks. So do you want to get your ribs X-rayed?"

"No, it's OK. They'd take me off flying status."

Later, some hundreds of dollars later, the insurance adjuster had called back twice to see if Brian hadn't injured himself that night.

No, he just did a parachute landing position fall, I had answered, not that the USAA insurance adjuster knew or cared. "You turn over on your back in the air, with all fours —arms and legs both up — and relax completely." That image had been affixed in the air as I turned my head back toward the on-ramp companion to the off-ramp exit we were taking to get onto the base. No wonder he had come home so often. This base looked as though it had nothing to it but rows of B-52s and a BOQ, the Bachelors' Officers Quarters.

Today we were all going to Merced. Bryan and his crew were already there. With me, driving, were Bryan's mother, his grandmother, and Kelly, who even at two years of age knew enough to wish she was staying home to play with friends. It was 108 degrees in the valley, and with no air conditioning in the old hot-rod Shelby, it was a relief to see the V-shaped wire entrance, wire-stenciled in dull green, of Merced Air Force Base. The California mountains were plastered to the back of the fence expanse in dimension-lacking flatness. We were all querulous. The sky was threatening rain; even this simmering monotone base would be a respite from the highway heat.

The grey mountains parted from the baseball diamond-high fence, as we drove onto the base. It did exist in more than x and y dimensions: a road wound its way toward the tipped-back mountains. The BOQ rooms on base were not much different from any puny motel room we had stayed in either discriminately or indiscriminately, over the years. It could be a seamy motel from anywhere; the slatted venetian blinds were closed against the sun. Things were not really so unusual: Bryan stood in his flight suit. The real life difference today was the airplane parked outside. It was difficult to ignore, bigger than the BOQ itself where Bryan and his crew had spent the night and about the size of a city block. I peered at him through the ripples of light and dark from the blinds, dead silence in the dank motel-like air, striped air I could see on the carpeting as well. It seemed he knew enough to be apprehensive, finally. It was the first time I had ever been able to tell at the moment of happening that he was, perhaps, scared. Usually if I knew it, it came in retrospect. His face was tense. I turned mine toward the tiny window, as though taking in the view.

Later, in December, after it had all happened, someone sent his briefcase to his original navigator Mike Bonvissuto, not knowing what else to do with it. Mike brought it over one day, and we emptied it together, starting with a B-52 training questionnaire that happened to be in it:

How many hours of aircraft commander time have you had?

Do you feel qualified as a B-52 Aircraft Commander as a result of your training?

Do you feel you could benefit from further time with a B-52 instructor pilot?

The answers had been "6 hours" of aircraft commander time, "No," to the adequacy of the training for being an aircraft commander and "No," to further benefit from flying with an instructor pilot. And the comment, in red ink by some B-52 instructor pilot, had been, "This guy must be either crazy or stupid."

I said to Mike, "Angry maybe — crazy or stupid — hardly." I laughed nonetheless, angry myself in retrospect, for what had come of it all and so quickly.

That July day of departure I was afraid to think much of anything, staring at him over the stripes of light. But I asked him straight out if he were nervous. He, of course, said no; this was a point we'd never been to before, not on any of our excursions. At the top of the Smokey mountains we had both wondered about sliding over the edge, but he had kept smiling. The same was true of the back sides of Yosemite and Yellowstone and of Highway 1 on the Pacific; we had driven many graveled and precipitously staged roads too fast. With the exception of my demand to be let out and my hitch-hiking stint on Alligator Alley, I had learned to wait for the predicaments, as I thought of them, to end safely. Now, the moment of what should have been reassurance on my part, came and went. Mental danger I could manage. Physical danger, if he was baffled, finally after all these years, then it was beyond me.

The months went by, December came, and we heard the crew would be home for a week, and that the week would actually include Christmas itself.

Bill had called me presumably before Bryan and the crew even knew on Guam. But just as surely as they came, they left. Bill had called Bryan to tell him first that they were being sent straight back. Things were in a pinch. They needed a Mather B-52, and it was tomorrow they needed it, back on Guam. Everyone except John was in the area.

Bryan called John and Ellen in Alabama where they were visiting their parents, picked John up at the airport later in the day and the two of them went to the base; meanwhile I picked up Bryan's mother at the airport, while John and Bryan were on base making arrangements for their departure that night at midnight from Merced. We set Christmas for the afternoon, I picked up John at his home on base at 6:00, and all of us — John, Bryan, Kelly, Bryan's mother and grandmother, my parents, Monica, and I — had Christmas drinks and dinner.

On this short notice, Ellen and their children had stayed in Alabama while John had taken the first available flight back. His house was dark when I picked him up. He was waiting at the door. He and Bryan played with Kelly while we finished fixing dinner, making balloon animals with her; an hour before midnight we drove to Merced. There was no talk of what was going on now over Hanoi. We all knew, and with both men, the one whom I knew well and the other whom I knew little, it was the same. Talking was an effort. The three of us rode silently in the dark following our own headlights on the now-deserted Route 99: I driving, Bryan in the front passenger seat, and John, in back. I hugged them both good-by on the runway; it was midnight on the nose, got into my car, and headed up 99 one more time.

Bryan said the runway at Guam was too short for a B-52; plus the end of it had a steep 600 ft drop-off from island to ocean. Maximum bomb-loaded B-52s used most of its 13,000 to 14,000 ft. to take-off. The image of B-52, close to a city block in size, landing or taking off on any runway, was always difficult for me. It seemed too large to fly, but easier to imagine once air-borne. Beyond Guam, one of the take-off points for B-52 crews flying to Vietnam, I had not imagined.

Now, approximately thirty-six hours later, Colonel Templeton and his cohorts, three of them, stood at my door, the blue color of their full dress uniforms and of the

Air Force station wagon, identical in color. Having gotten to my front porch in an instant, I stood still; I watched them emerge from the station wagon. I had seen the official vehicle heading up my street, ever so slowly along the row of huge palms toward the river bluff, an incline that took them out of view from my window. I leaned hard on my kitchen counter, on tiptoes of bare feet with my elbows locked, and wondered what an official Air Force station wagon was doing in a residential neighborhood.

I peered past the palms. The wagon was backing down the black-topped incline, and in the moment it became evident that their search was concluded at my house.

"I'm afraid I have some bad news for you." Colonel Templeton was standing closer to my front door than I, and I moved in on it, putting my hand on the knob.

"I'm sorry, but you can't come in, " I said.

"We have to come in," the Colonel was speaking again, saying once more that he was sorry.

"But I have my whole family and Bryan's whole family here, you just can't come in. They can't know. They're not all well."

Conceding, I opened the door while I wondered what he would have done had I really refused. I felt both my hands in the back pockets of my jeans now - my fingertips pushing at the bottom seams. I glanced at our two mothers, past the fireplace. Each, as though in a painting, it struck me even then, was seated in a chair in the opposite far corners of the living room. They knew too. Poised for the moment, as though for a social call, Christmas not yet over, they seemed to arise and come forward simultaneously in their bright dresses.

I stepped between them and the colonel, feeling my elbows jutting in all directions, trying not to poke him or my mother standing closest, and with my fingers pushing hard in my back pockets now, I stopped him from saying it aloud.

"It is not too surprising, is it?" I posed. "Losses are about as the Pentagon predicted, so I hear, one in four or five." It hadn't even been two days since I had dropped Bryan and John off at Merced. I went on with the whole purpose of my saying it. Bill had told me the flying facts just this morning. "What else can you expect for flying straight and level over Hanoi?"

The Colonel looked at me, wondering, I was sure, both at my information and at my stating it. I cringed a bit, but it mattered less that it wasn't his fault than that it had happened. Somehow we all moved into the living room. My father appeared and Monica, Bryan's grandmother and Kelly. Then, crouching down, I told Kelly as best I could what Colonel had finally told our mothers. There was no way to hide it. The news was out now, had been all morning without my knowing it, on base: the gas station, the commissary, BX, hospital, everyone was talking about it. A B-52 would have to be sent to replace the one that had been sent to replace the other.

"No beepers and no 'chutes," was how the Colonel stated the reports from the B-52s following Bryan's which had witnessed the whole thing. There was no sign of survival according to those crews. The Colonel by the end of the afternoon had said it a number of times to us all, more than once to me. Having heard him the first time, I asked him to repeat it. The B-52s following had not seen or heard a thing, and there had been a lot of them following. They had, in fact, seen it blow up but no one told anyone that until later. The crew just had not gotten out. The pilot, co-pilot, and electronics warfare officer were supposed to eject upwards. The radar navigator and the navigator were to eject downwards, and the gunner was to jump physically through a manually operated hatch beside his seat.

Finally they left. I had told the chaplain I had nothing to ask him or to say to him after he made an offer to help. I knew that it was not his fault either, but that also mattered little now. The flight surgeon left his home telephone number; Colonel Templeton said once again to my father and our mothers how sorry he was, and to me. Then they left. In the night my German shepherd suddenly lunged and barked; it was 5 AM, just the paper boy. I let him out and he ran for the paper. I hated the feel of the damp cold, even in California.

There was plenty of light to see by. The moon was full and white, small as a bleached penny. The San Francisco Chronicle headlines said it — A Northern California-Based B-52 Shot Down Over Hanoi — the article below stated that the crew was presumed dead.   Damp darkness sank in over me. The terror I had dreaded, came and sat in another layer, a diver's black wetsuit: skin-tight and suffocating. Maybe if I had thought beyond the runway on Guam, it would have helped. There were two hours until daylight. My feet hung off one end of the couch as I lay back down, my arms off the other end, and I was holding Smokey by the collar. The sun came up, and in the light I could see my sister's and my daughter's forms in blankets beside him on the living room floor.

11

PORK-FAT VERSUS FAT-BACK

At breakfast Monica said she had dreamed about Bryan. In it, she had seen him crouched in bushes; she was sure he was alive; sure, sure, I said, and I half believed it. More than that, Bryan's life forte was survival; we had neither Rambo nor cult survivalists in those days. He just did things alone to test his physical ability to survive and it was sometimes, now being an exception, a source of contention between us.

His theory was that physical risks were more profound, and therefore to be undertaken more seriously, than mental risks. He had started early in life, when he was three, climbing high in the treetops beyond the reach of anyone, and his grandmother had then fixed him up in a woman's slip for playing outside so that he would be too mortified to cause another stir of the kind that would require the attendance of a fire squad and truck.

Now Monica was repeating her dream, sitting cross-legged by the fireplace with Bill. I silently regretted that this had been Bryan's opportunity to test his endurance. It was noon. Bill's movie star smile flashed. He was trying hard, "If I know Bryan, he will be in downtown Hanoi right now."

Possible enough, we all concurred. It could easily be true, if he'd been able to eject and able to survive the ejection.

I talked to the other wives: Renee, married to Michael, the navigator; Ellen married to John, the electronics warfare officer; Sally, married to the gunner, David Gavin. We had not met one another in person; Rich, the copilot, was a bachelor. We did not know if he had a girlfriend, and never having met the radar navigator, we knew less even about him. I talked to Ellen in the day following my notification. A military official had come from the base in Huntsville to notify her and their mutual families: John's mother, his brother: his family and hers in Pinehurst, North Carolina. She said that she would return the following day and had already arranged for a friend to meet her up at the airport All of the rest of us lived close by, here in California. The local paper and national news services called. Radio stations called for telephone interviews, and the telephone continued to ring regularly. Bryan's mother and mine kept order, and among us as crew members' families, we came to believe we were being tapped. We began, over the static, watching what we said to one another.

At the end of the week a friend of Bryan's from pilot training, called from Randolph Air Force Base in San Antonio, Texas. After our hellos he explained that he was stationed at the Casualty Center. His position was working in intelligence, gathering information that related to captured and missing airmen. He was on duty now.

"As soon as I saw Bryan's name on the list, I started keeping really close track of the intelligence," he said. "Listen, Layne, a set of photos of six guys just came through from Japanese intelligence." I felt him hesitate. "I'm almost afraid to say this because I'm just not sure myself, but one of these guys looks like Bryan to me, or at least sort of like Bryan."

"Really?" I asked and we both paused.

"If it would be OK with you, I'd like to send it out and have you take a look at it."

I said, "I think so. Send it along." He sent it to the base and Bill brought it. We all looked, passing the composite set of xerox snapshots around our group of family and friends as we lined up in the living room on the couch and on the floor beside it. I knew which photo Jim meant. It was the head that would belong to a figure that would be, if viewable in a full figure, slightly smaller than most. The close-cropped hair could easily be Bryan's. Beyond that, I was somewhat puzzled.

Everyone kept handing the sheet back to me, perhaps for my making a final collective decision. But I just couldn't be certain. The face was darkened both by the photocopying and by what would now be, if it were Bryan, three days' growth of beard. The questionable head was turned slightly, narrowing its cross-dimensions even more. My best assurance that it was Bryan was that the face portion that was visible and the semi-profile looked hauntingly so much like him that it would be difficult to image this photo being someone else. The visage, whosoever it truly was, looked incredibly gaunt; in ordinary time that change would have taken months.

The next day confirmation came for three of the six of the crew. Again, it was Jim Wyandotte who called to tell me that Bryan, David, and Rich were alive and had been taken as POWs. There was no word on John, Randy, or Michael. We all talked on the phone more. How if Bryan and Rich, upstairs in the plane, and David in the back, had been able to get out, that it was likely they'd all gotten out. But we weren't very convinced. We speculated about all that might have happened when it got hit by a SAM: we did not know then that there was some confusion by aircraft following as to its being hit by one, possibly two, or even three SAMS simultaneously. We talked more about the static and interferences on our lines. We noted that it doubled approximately when we talked with one another, and we talked again about being tapped, by whom we weren't sure, perhaps the FBI.

The first week passed and the turn of the year came, and with it, the close of the war, January 11, 1973. In the staggered releases of POWs, during the months of February and March, Bryan's crew came last, March 30th of that year.

Pork-fat or fat-back, what was it Bryan had said in our greeting upon his own release? I had tried time and again to remember that two sentence conversation between him and Jim Frommer, a B-52 gunner whom I had heard Bryan talk about for weeks. He knew that Jim and I would really get along, he said, and was really looking forward to our meeting one another.

Soon enough, I had seen a man who fit Bryan's description of Jim in the base library one afternoon. Standing, he was reading at the magazine rack. Occasionally he looked in the direction of the table where I was seated, as I looked in his, and I went home and told Bryan that I had met Jim Frommer.

Jim described himself as being butterscotch in color. He said the reason was that he was half-white and half-black. We learned that he had been the smartest kid to ever graduate from his high school in Illinois. Even Bryan didn't say that about himself, but we both believed Jim to be telling the truth.

How Jim had ever come to be in the Air Force was rather a question. He had been promoted as far as he could and was now the highest grade sergeant possible. But his sarcasm on the subject of the U.S. government, The War, and Nixon were endless. He referred to Bryan upon occasion, as Nixon's hatchet man. He played wonderful basketball, wore the original pair of tinted glasses that turned translucent tan in the sun to match his skin, and read constantly, standing or sitting.

We stood in line, the day Bryan came home, in the lobby of Travis Air Force Base terminal, with an enormous crowd outside. Only families and close friends were allowed into the terminal, but the base had been partially opened to the public and the flight line was crowded with expectant well-wishers. The last C-141 transport of the ex-POWs had landed here in Northern California; Bryan and the others had emerged from the plane, ducking from the sun and waving and following hugs and kisses from all, they had then been escorted into waiting Air Force vehicles to disappear behind the flight line. They were then to meet their families again in the lobby.

Arrangements had been made for eight of us to greet Bryan in the lobby. There were Bryan's mother, Kelly, and I, and Bill, my so-called escort officer, for this welcoming portion of the arrival; and there were friends Mike, Bryan's original navigator and his wife, Diane, plus Jim and Roweena Frommer.

Now all of us were lined up along a rope that had been temporarily rigged for cordoning off a walkway into the lobby from a nearby hanger. I was no less apprehensive than anyone else among us. We had already hugged briefly outside as he disembarked from the cargo plane, Bryan and Kelly and I, and with Bill opening and closing doors, we went into the lobby; then Bryan had disappeared with the others. There were about ten of them altogether on this flight into the U.S. Now he appeared again. There was the initial awkwardness which was predictable, but then I couldn't seem to speak. I remembered his landing on a commercial flight from a visit to his father's in Yemen, a Masai spear in hand. We hadn't mentioned it until we were at the car, trying to find a place for it — his waiting until I couldn't resist saying something about it anymore. When I had finally acknowledged that he was carrying an unusual parcel, he had told me profusely about how angry he was at its having gotten bent, despite protective wrapping, in the course of his flights from Africa through New York to

Indiana. Refraining from commenting on purpose was what I wished for now.

"You look like hell." It was Jim Frommer, standing at the head of our line, across the rope from Bryan. He reached across the rope for Bryan's shoulders with both hands. "What did they feed you over there or did they feed you at all?"

From beyond the roped row of us, Bryan answered Jim without a pause: "Something you would really have liked," he said. "Fat-back. They tried to make it into a soup."

Which was it, pork-fat, or fat-back, that he said? It took me ten years to remember. *Webster's fat-back: the strip of fat taken from the upper part of a side of pork and usually dried and salt-cured, eaten in the South by the blacks.* Bryan had let us all off the hook of embarrassment for himself; he and Jim were together again. The diminution had started in those first three days of the intelligence photo; out of our midst, he had lived with its continuance. His hair, close to auburn in July was nearly white this following March. Jim asked what he weighed. He said 130 lbs, and then to all of us, in an addressing manner and looking at us straight, he said that he knew he looked thin but that we shouldn't worry about it. They had told him in the Philippines that he was fine except for worms. We laughed and felt our eyes cracking at the corners with the warmth of having him with us again. We all relied on him for something. In the Officers' Quarters, rummaging through the suitcase that I had brought with me for some Levis, he found a pair, pulled them on and then stared at me. The legs — I looked down — were too long.

It was not just a question of shrinking on top of dwindling. It was partly the jeans. We were the inverse of each other: 28 and 34, inseam or waist, depending upon which of us it was, and we were the inverse of a normal couple. I was taller and he was shorter. It was my jeans that he had on. Rolling them up, he put his arms around his mother and me and carrying Kelly now, we all got into the big silver Pontiac Bill had sold us for $50 and went off to McDonald's just outside the base gate, his first choice of things that he wanted to do. We drove up and down Interstate 80, kidding about driving on in to San Francisco to the left, or on up to Lake Tahoe to the right, from the base; finally, we turned the car around to come back to the base. They had given him an hour before checking officially into the hospital.

12

WHAT HE TOLD ME

___ The Hanoi Hilton

At the end of the Vietnam War
Back in December of '72
The U.S. Gov't bombed Hanoi
Using one hundred B-52s.

The reasons for the bombing are over.
The facts remaining are these:
Statisticians have calculated losses
At 25,000 of Vietnamese.

Now one day an error was made
As the bombers came through the sky.
Instead of their military target,
They struck the hospital, Bach Mai.

And on the steps of that same hospital
Joanie Baez still stands and sings,
In a voice high, sweet, and beautiful,
Of B-52s, war criminals, and things.

But listen, my friends, and I'll tell you
A story that has yet to see light,
Of dark figures, war criminal phantoms,
POWs who prayed for bombs in the night.

The story among them is told
Of torture so out of sight
That the sound of the bombing was like music,
And they cheered in their courtyard that night.

News Services' Information.   As the close of the U.S. involvement in the Vietnam War in late 1972 neared, a deadlock in negotiations between the North Vietnamese and U.S. governments occurred in December, 1972, as reported by Secretary of State Henry Kissinger. Subsequently, B-52 bombings of Hanoi and Haiphong were carried out December 18 through December 29. Negotiations were resumed on a technical level January 3rd and on a substantive level, January 8th, according to Secretary Kissinger. The signing of the Paris Peace Agreement took place January 11th, 1973.

The return of the POWs was initiated following the signing of the Paris Peace Agreement. The repatriation occurred in stages over a period of time from January 30 to March 30th, in approximately two-week intervals.

A listing of 555 POWs to be returned to the U.S. was provided by the North Vietnamese following the Paris Agreement. The order of return, however, was stipulated by the POWs and agreed upon by both governments. This listing was published at the time of the first group's release, January 30th, 1973.

Shootdowns. The order of return specified by the POWs was the reverse order of shootdown date. Captain John Alvarez, F-105 pilot captured in December of 1967, was the first POW to return to the U.S., January 30, 1973. B-52 tail gunner, Sergeant David Gavin, B-52 co-pilot, Captain Rich Cunningham, and B-52 aircraft commander, Captain Bryan Martin, captured December 26th, 1972, were the last POWs to be returned, March 30th, 1973.

Logistically, at each interval those POWs in outlying camps including Dog Patch, the Zoo, the Plantation, Las Vegas, and others, were transported in small groups by the North Vietnamese centrally into Hanoi and gathered at the Hanoi Hilton, an old French prison, now nick-named "The Hilton" by U.S. prisoners-of-war. From Hanoi, they were flown out by U.S. transport planes, permitted into the Gia Lam Airport on designated days by the North Vietnamese Government for that purpose.

All POWs were flown first to Clark Air Force Base in the Philippines where they were hospitalized. Medical examinations and intelligence debriefings were undertaken. The purpose of the debriefings was that of obtaining all possible information from the POWs themselves concerning unaccounted for crew members and to combine it with information gathered from other intelligence sources in order to determine as accurately as possible the fate of the missing.

Following three days at Clark Air Force Base, the Military Air Command then further flew the ex-POWs to the formerly assigned base of each or to the base on which the respective family was living.

2,118 airmen were killed in the air war over Vietnam. Following the return of 555 POWs, March 30, l973, in numbers no more nor less than initially listed by the North Vietnamese Government, 2558 men remained missing in action.

Armageddon. The many descriptions by the POWs held in the Hanoi Hilton during the time of the last bombings of the Vietnam War — these came to be known as the Christmas Bombings — have one element in common: from the beginning of the bombings, approximately midnight of December 18th, the prisoners had a certainty, because the B-52s had come to Hanoi, that the war would soon come to an end. The impact of the bombing upon the Hanoi environs itself was described from two aspects in all accounts: as a literal shaking of the earth's surface accompanied by blinding light brighter than daylight. The POWs had not known of these bombings by any previously transmitted information from incoming prisoners. However, the Hanoi Hilton prisoners-of-war, prior to the knowledge of their North Vietnamese guards and interrogators and prior to the impact of the bombs themselves, knew by sound, that the B-52s were in Hanoi.

Whether the watch tower served electronically in a manner analogous to a lightening rod, as one suggestion had it, to protect the Hanoi Hilton itself from the bombing, is not known. What was known, as far as the POWs were concerned, was that the eleven days of Christmas Bombings by the B-52s, described by one POW as Armageddon for the North Vietnamese, brought about the end of the war for the U.S. and the subsequent release of the North Vietnamese held U.S. POWs.

What Brian Told. Inside the Hanoi Hilton on the night of December 26th, the survivors of the B-52 crew were interrogated about other crew members. At that time the tail gunner, copilot, and pilot had seen one another in the transit by truck from the crash site, 20 miles northwest of Hanoi, to the city.

Bryan said that during the first interrogation he was certain that a nearby scream he heard was from his electronics warfare officer, John Dearborn. Recognizing what he thought was John's voice, that left one crew member, Michael Clark — the navigator, unaccounted for in the Hanoi Hilton.

Later that night, interrogations were repeated and were again focused on crew member credentials. The North Vietnamese asked Bryan to repeat the names, ranks, and flying positions of all of his crew members. Upon refusal, he was blindfolded, tied in a chair and told that he would be given until the count of ten to divulge the name specifically of his electronics warfare officer. He refused by telling the interrogators that they planned to kill him anyway, and therefore it did not matter that he did not answer their questions.   A gun was put to his head, the counting was started and then stopped at the count of nine. Bryan was then informed that the name of this crew member was already known to his interrogators. It was stated by one of the interrogators that the electronics warfare officer was a black man by the name of Major John Dearborn. The interview was terminated, and Bryan was placed in solitary confinement.

His conclusion from the interrogation was that the North Vietnamese intelligence sources were not likely to have had possession of the information concerning his crew roster. Bryan told me he believed, instead, that the North Vietnamese had John in their possession whether dead or alive.

At the time of their being shot down, the impact by the SAM, possibly two, even three SAMs, according to crew members in the B-52s following in the same flight of planes, occurred from the right side where Michael's position was located. B-52s following saw it burst into flame and blow in the air prior to its hitting the ground.

The chain of events, from John's first statement of an all clear on radar and his subsequent swearing and stating that they were going to take a hit, to Bryan's own order for bail-out, occurred within seconds. Bryan said that from the time that the forward cockpit canopy blew, to the time that he was taken in on the truck by the North Vietnamese, midnight by Greenwich mean time, he could recollect nothing except hitting the ground.

During the entire time in prison, there was no subsequent word or evidence of either John or Michael.

In solitary confinement for what was termed his bad attitude, Bryan spent the first month in a single cell. There was a door to the right side of the cell that opened into what he presumed was a neighboring cell. He could hear voices on the opposite side and found that the individuals, three of them, were English speaking, assumedly other POWs. The door was nailed shut.

Using his fingers, it took three days for him to work the nails from the margins of the door itself. He took it off late at night, so as not to be seen doing it by the guards, only to find a larger cell that housed one Caucasian and two Oriental men. He assumed immediately that it was a set up. He said nothing to them about it, while he made himself take three more days to determine in his own mind whether they were, in fact, American pilots or North Vietnamese interrogators.

One man said that his hometown was Auburn, California, just north of Sacramento. Through the door, the two discussed restaurants over the state of California, Bryan's way of quizzing the voice for the purpose of determining in his own mind that Gordy Nakagawa was, as Bryan learned, Japanese-American. Both Gordy Nakagawa and Jim Nagahero were, in fact, Japanese-American Navy pilots stationed in San Diego. Having affirmed their identity as Americans, Bryan then removed the door every night to join the others while the guards were not in attendance, replacing it nightly before sun-up.

Collectively they and the others recently shot down, most notably those taken captive during the B-52 bombing raids in the week immediately past, were known in the prison as the New Guys. The Old Guys, some of whom had been held in prison, six, seven, and eight years, were highly revered by those B-52 crew members just taken prisoner, or New Shootdowns as they were also called among the other prisoners. In turn, the B-52 crews were heroes to the Old Guys. There was no question among the other Hanoi inmates: the B-52 jocks had saved their lives, they said, and they had known that they could.

When the B-52s came to Hanoi, it was the terrified

guards who hid from the cataclysm of the raining bombs while the Old Shootdowns cried and cheered in the compound yard. Treatment by the guards improved within the first day. And treatment, according to the experienced POWs, was always indicative, as by a rippling from the top down, of the tenor of attitude by the North Vietnamese government.

Among the American imprisoned, the code of conduct had been established and practiced by the Old Shootdowns. In the remaining days of prison for them and the beginning days for the B-52 crews, there were new self-regulations. Either all were to go home, or none would go; there would be no agreement by them as a collective body for a partial release and there would be no pre-release of any POWs. In the name of fairness to the Old Guys, the sequence of release would not be alphabetical or by rank, with the exception of those severely injured and requiring medical attention, but would be the inverse order of shoot-down dates. The Old Guys were to go first, and the B-52 crews, last.

With the beginning of the POW release, the men were given new clothes: dark shirts and pants, grey windbreakers, and black shoes made from rubber tires. The North Vietnamese wanted them to look good, going home. Despite anticipation, none was confident that their mutual release would actually be accomplished until it occurred. However, with each agreed-upon date, the U.S. Military Air Command C-140 transports flew into Hanoi, picked up the POWs, and took off from Hanoi in clockwork fashion. Meanwhile, the POWs, having been brought from outlying camps into the Hilton, cleaned up, and loaded onto buses, were taken to Gia Lam to meet the C-140s, with those behind waiting carefully in turn.

The day of the last release, March 30, CBS News with Walter Cronkite was allowed into Hanoi on one of the C-140s. Bryan and David had been brought to the Hanoi Hilton prison from an outlying prison, called the Zoo. It was located on the outskirts of Hanoi. There they were housed in a section of the Zoo called the Pig Stye. At the Hanoi Hilton where they had spent the night, both said they did not recognize Walter Cronkite when he entered the cell in the morning, just prior to their departure. It took a few moments for them to realize that it was a U.S. television crew and Cronkite in person. Cronkite was portlier in real life than on television. They, in fact, had not known of their release date until it literally came upon them that moment as they were being taken, in the last group of POWs, to the buses.

I said to Bryan, "Yes, we saw it on TV. I saw you duck from the cameras. It made me believe that you had been tortured."

"It wasn't for that reason. We thought it was North Vietnamese television. None of us was to be seen on it."

I went on, "Then getting on the bus, someone at the end even asked Walter who had won the Super Bowl."

"That was me," he said.

"I should have known," I said.

Then I added, "Did you know that you were the last POW released?" Bryan looked puzzled. "They announced it that all the way from Hanoi, when Walter said it,   to California , when you landed. I was afraid they might keep just one — it would have been you — for bargaining."

13

SUMMER OF THE INDY 500

The following summer of 1973 we went to President Nixon's dinner at the White House for all of the POWs, Governor Reagan's dinner in Sacramento for all the California Air Force and Navy POWs, and dinner for Indiana POWs given by Indiana's Governor Bowen. Governor Bowen's dinner was before the 500 Mile Race in Indianapolis, and all POWs and their families were to be guests of the Governor's at the Indianapolis 500 itself.

Governor Bowen was a physician who had practiced for years in a small town in northern Indiana. Now elected Governor, he and his family had moved to Indianapolis and were living in the Riley Towers, a tall pair of buildings with apartments on the top floors. The Governor and his family had apparently decided not to live in what we knew as the Governor's Mansion on Meridian Avenue. Located in the next block from the house Susan and I had rented from Mr. Haverford of the elevator company, all we knew about the mansion itself, aside from its now being in what was becoming an integrated neighborhood, hence Mr. Haverford's buying the block of houses, was that the Governor's mansion was ancient and had gold-plated toilet seats, so rumor had it for all of our growing up years.

Maybe the Governor made a special point of grilling the steaks himself, that night, on the grill of his balcony, so many stories up. The Bowens' apartment was on the uppermost floor of the Riley Towers, so the veranda that spanned the width of the apartment, was open above to the stars. At dinner, we sat at a table for four with a POW who had been interred for eight years. He was one of the famous ones, Bryan told me afterwards. The ex-POW spoke of his pet rats. I looked across what was the balcony of the apartment, at Governor Bowen. I knew he was an MD, and I was, after all, a biologist. I probably knew more about rats than anyone here. The stars cluttering the sky moved edgeward, perceptibly in concert; I looked again and drew courage from Governor Bowen.

"So, could you say what it was actually like," I asked, speaking to the famous POW, "Living with rats for so long?"

He answered me easily, the stars at his back: "It was terrible, at first. and then," he said, " I had to get used to it. I named them, and I learned to live with them. They were the only company I had for awhile."

The next day at the 500 Mile Race we sat with the celebrities. We had already been to the reception with them in a downtown hotel. There were few people at the hotel when we all arrived in our open convertibles. We had actually been sitting on the seat backs as we rode in a downtown Indianapolis parade. The movie stars had apparently arrived at the hotel in their convertibles earlier, and they were gathered in a room next door to the room reserved for race drivers and ex-POWs. Bryan sat down in a chair while I wandered around looking. When I came back, he was talking to someone shorter than he whom I had seen come in the door earlier, walking with a slight limp. He seemed very young. Maybe he knew a good thing when he saw it and had walked in from off the street.   You could see all the food, tables of it, from the windows, and no one was paying any attention to those entering at the door. I saw the pale blond person walking toward the row of chairs with a plate of food as I came back around again to sit down.

"Hi," he was sitting down next to Bryan," How're you doing."

"Just fine, I think." Bryan leaned his chair up on its back legs. "Are you here for the race?"

"Yes, I am. You too?"

"Roger. We came in last night," Bryan answered matter-of-factly.

"I thought I'd get something to eat. It looks pretty good."

"I know.   We were just talking about having something ourselves." Bryan looked over at me.

"So what do you do?" The young man perhaps thought that Bryan was a race car driver.

"Oh, I fly airplanes. How about you?"

" Yeah, I drive cars," the blond person stated.

"That's one thing I've always wanted to do," said Bryan, "But I've just never taken the time. Maybe I'll think about that this fall."

"Really. I've been thinking about learning to fly lately. Something I've always wanted to do too."

The two seemed to be in agreement, and their conversation ended as the din of noise rising in the room was beginning to make conversation difficult. The room was filled by now, and people were still coming in the door. Apparently the celebrities' party across the hotel lobby was over, and they were coming in here for the refreshments. Someone pointed out the Allison brothers.

I said to one of the men who was acting as both chauffeur and organizer for the entourage. "Could you tell me who that person is Bryan was talking to?" The chauffeur organizer person had been ubiquitous all week-end from brunch through dinner and now for the race, and was standing off to the side of the row of chairs.

"Do you know who he is?" I repeated my question. I wondered at such a quiet conversation between him and Bryan in the midst of all of this hullabaloo for the race. Maybe he had really just come in off the street and would disappear just as unnoticed. The man answered me with his voice rising a notch in pitch, "Don't you know?" he exclaimed. "That's Mark Donahue. He's an Indy 500 race driver. He won it last year. He's more famous than most. Plus he's an engineer and he does his own race car designing."

No, I didn't know. Of course not. I was, it was true, what was called a Hoosier. This was my home state, but I had never been to the 500. When I lived in Indianapolis I knew enough to stay off the streets the day of the race, and I'd had a medical school lab partner who rode the ambulance for the race. That was it. There were the Allison brothers at the buffet, where someone had just pointed them out to me. Bryan and Mr. Donahue were another pair, smaller than average in stature and barely audible in their conversation. I wondered, less than idly, how much more physical fortitude could be contained in a pair than in these two, Bryan and Mark Donahue, and whether such parties recognized each other automatically in that quietness of tone and manner of small-talk speaking, or whether it was just the opposite: that they never recognized one another. Only we, who were different from them, recognized them. I stepped into the crowd near the table where Bryan was now standing. He was looking my way. "You'll never believe who you were just talking to," I said. "Did you know who he was?"

"No, should I?"

"Well, yes.   You'll be amazed.   That was Mark Donahue."

"Really! That *is* amazing."

14

NO NEWS

Upon the release of the POWs the information concerning Major John Dearborn, Bryan's electronics warfare officer, was no more complete than it had been from the time of the remaining crew members being taken captive. Circumstances surrounding what had happened to him, whether or not he had bailed out of the airplane, whether or not he was taken captive along with the rest, alive as Bryan had thought, were no more clear than the night that Bryan was interrogated concerning his crew.

Ellen Johnson, John's wife, waited with the rest of us, hoping that in the last release of prisoners, John would somehow appear. When he did not and after Bryan told her what he knew, Ellen went back to North Carolina to be with John's family and with her own. In the fall, she returned, and then, she and her children moved to Seattle to take a teaching position in an elementary school there, saying she had a brother who lived close. She called once. I called her back twice.

From that time, she disappeared from our lives and, unfortunately, we did not stop her.

15

INDIAN SUMMER

In early October of that year, 1973, six months after the return of Bryan's crew, the Air Force notified Renee Clark, Michael Clark's parents, and Bryan that the North Vietnamese were returning Michael's body. We drove to a mortuary in Oakland, the land-side of the San Francisco Bay, where Bryan went in to identify Michael's body and to make arrangements for his transport to a family burial place in Utah.

Tell me the end of innocence cannot be repeated: we had come from the East, these Californians thought. Anything East of the Rockies was East. Never mind that. Here death was in a West Coast performance, and Bryan had stood to lose again, now two of the three best friends he had made: Bill, his instructor-pilot, was still living, Mike's death was certain and John, if not dead, was lost to us all: both were now gone. And I wondered, even knowing it would have to be possible, how Bryan would possibly live. He was putting Mike's dog tags into his pocket as he climbed into the car.

Later in the week, we went to the home of Mike's parents in Stockton, California, where we gathered with all of his family and friends: his sisters and nieces and nephews, along with with his parents, for a service in his honor. Stockton had come to call: friends, teachers, neighbors, professional associates of his parents, too many relatives alone to count. The service in which the family minister spoke about Mike's younger years and Bryan spoke of their flying time together, was held in the Mormon church in Stockton.

We went back to the home of the Clark's following the service. His father, a man of 6'7" stood at the doorway in a home built for himself and his family; it had the appearance of a huge log cabin, looking more than two stories high and more than a single-house wide. His own appearance was one more of a frontiersman than of the psychologist that he was. His mother, a teacher in the Stockton schools, made us feel welcome in their family comforting others, all of us, more than the reverse. Renee, Bryan, and I went to Mike's room, where we sat crouched together for awhile on the bottom mattress of his bunk bed, thinking and talking of him. Like his father, Mike had been very tall, 6'4", dwarfing Renee who was barely five feet tall, and now, the thought of his tall presence loomed corner-to-corner in what would have been a small room for him. Together, we and his family had comforted one another with the knowledge Mike had always wanted to fly more than anything in the world. His room, full of flying memorabilia and model airplanes, made it too much to speak of now: driving home Bryan murmured, more to himself than to me, that he would never fly anything but a single-seater again.

16

THE AFTERTHOUGHT

AUGUST, 1988

Somehow things just hadn't and weren't coming out right. In fact, in those few years since his being an undergrad at Purdue and my quitting medical school, things had gone out of control. Bryan had been to Vietnam two times, for almost as many years, and I was in limbo. A few short years, it was the cross-ever between the 60's and 70's. They were the years of the hippies — I mocked them for their general naivete; Bryan, who couldn't get beyond the war with them, mocked them for their being naively anti-war. My mother-in-law, I'm sure, was afraid I was a closet hippie, fearful that I would, in the long run, emerge one day in my jeans, embarrassing them all and thereby ruining what was to become Bryan's career in the Air Force. My friends were afraid they had lost me to the military; they couldn't believe that I had gone to a dinner given by Richard Nixon. I didn't know what I was. We had been married more than five years before I ever conceded to buying furniture and that only at the death of Bryan's grandmother, who had left him something of a small inheritance. Bryan was the same. We had agreed on that.

Now it is the 90s - even the time of the yuppies has come and gone. I crouch beneath the beach house, feet planted in line with the stilts, eavesdropping, and listening to the sounds of feet on the planks, down the wooden steps and then squeaking in the sand, thinking there finally may be a secret I missed, a small one to make all the difference and spare me a lot of time. It's not that I hate them, exactly. I just want the middle of my own life back. I blame the war, but it's not altogether the war's fault either. I have saved myself over and over, this way and that. Perhaps I could have become a yuppie. I could have passed for a hippie, after all. Whatever: a whole-hearted plunge into something, an oblivion of sorts, and I might not have had to undergo all that repetitious self-saving.

We, too, were wonderful as undergrads. Bryan at Purdue, an engineering school, refused to join all those engineers; instead, he majored one at a time, in every other science, going up the pillar from pre-med, to biology, to chemistry, to math, and finally to physics. On a drugstore stool he had told me he wanted to be an astronaut; Willie

Ley and his rockets were to become a familiar topic and Purdue hadn't yet borne its fourteen astronauts. And for me, there I was in medical school, ten women in a class of 200, in those days as well. Bryan was my best buddy. One day he stole a pink slip from the secretary in the Dean's office, wrote a notification that I was flunking anatomy and should make an appointment with the Dean, and we both ran away from school for just a time.

Now I miss the Air Force sometimes. I miss its sand-colored life. I can feel the shade-cool liquidy stripes of sand running through me in hour-glass streams. They are pale yellow and creamy gray, and the noise of the jets keeps me calm: caustic runways of asphalt and cement, turning into flat sand color where the real sand starts. Nothing but rows and rows of jet airplanes and hangers, every air training base the same: looking up, the sky feels like an upside-down ground in its noise; it was all a safe umbrella under which to hide. And the ground beneath one's feet was always desert-warm.

Except for the officers' clubs, even in the minutes required for check cashing, I learned to drive around them all, like cesspools, on every base. Officers' wives clubs luncheons, the reminders that I had quit medical school, ambivalent as I had been, this was hardly better with those whiteclothed tables in darkened air-conditioning where I knew I could never sit long enough, despite the cool, to get through a whole luncheon. Tacitly, I came to understand that I could ruin Bryan's potential career that way too, by not attending.

I live in the country now—in my jeans and sweatshirts. Sometimes I put on my black wool suit with its wide black belt and pleated skirt: And I go into town in my black Laser car to do business, the ultimate hippie-yuppie amalgam, armored from having to save myself again I hope, planning to get through the rest of my life in some similar fashion, in fact, grateful that I don't have to live the middle of my life right now after all.

17

SR-71 TITANIUM BLACKBIRD

After returning from Vietnam, Bryan spent some months trying to decide what he wanted to do. He talked about going into the SR-71 program at Beale Air Force base forty miles north of Sacramento and about going to test pilot school south on the Mojave at Edwards Air Force Base. Prior to the Space Shuttle landings, Edwards Air Force Base was known to the general public from occasional stories in the news media about some test pilot in another new airplane, one bearing little resemblance to those seen in public airports and usually breaking an already short-lived record of speed or maneuverability. Quite the opposite was true of Beale Air Force Base. It was next to nonexistent on the map. During the Eisenhower administration Francis Gary Powers had been shot down over the Soviet Union in the U-2 spy plane and although his capture and subsequent release became news, the U.S. public knew little about it except that Powers himself was held in prison briefly by the Russians. The little-discussed U-2 was the forerunner to the SR-71 blackbird, as it was called by those who flew it. It was not an everyday topic of flying conversation even for pilots.

Bryan and I talked about getting out of the Air Force. He had an application from Eastern Airlines. There the pilots had collectively made a blanket invitation to any POW who wanted to retire from the Air Force or Navy and fly again. Collectively also, the cable car operators in San Francisco had offered their jobs to returning POWs.

Later in the summer Bryan went for an interview at the University of California School of Medicine, San Francisco; following it, they said they would accept him. He had an undergraduate degree that had already gotten him into medical school once and he could start in the fall.

We had agreed we both wanted to stay in California, preferably Northern California. Test pilot school or SR-71 training both meant we could stay in Sacramento, and I could go to graduate school at the University of California at Davis, 40 miles west toward San Francisco. The same was true of medical school at UC San Francisco. I had already been accepted at UC Davis for the fall term, 1973. My application and acceptance had occurred over the summer while Brian was trying to make his own decision.

Meanwhile Bryan perfunctorily began the Eastern application. Mid-summer, I found it on the dining room table half filled-out and I asked him what he thought, about flying for the airlines. "I really don't care to be a bus driver in the sky," was his response.

"Is that so much different from being an aluminum overcast?" I asked, using his way of referring to flying B-52s. "Besides, you would make a lot of money doing it now." I half-smiled.

It was becoming apparent that he had no intention of completing the Eastern application. I decided to make a point of the unfinished application. I didn't really care one way or the other about Eastern itself. "So what would be so terrible about flying four hours a month. That's all you say you would have to do." Clearly he thought flying an airliner was beneath him. I was tired of our mutual ambivalence. "You could lie around and read the whole rest of the time."

A few days later when the subject came up again, I asked him about going to graduate school in physics. He had always talked of doing it *when* he got out of the Air Force. That was becoming a question. I was beginning to think it differently, *if* he got out of the Air Force. At Purdue, it had never occurred to me that we would, in fact, stay in the Air Force. We had been in the Air Force five years now, one year longer than his commitment from his draft stipulation. In frustration one day, I asked it he would be willing to go to graduate school with no support from anyone. "We could do it," I said as we were discussing what was becoming the same old topic, "If we wanted it badly enough."

"You've always hated the Air Force," he said without

looking at me.

I said, "That's not fair and you know it." Still he didn't look at me, and I was wondering if he was going to carry on without looking at me altogether. I resumed talking before he could interject more. "You say that, but who do you know, what wife besides me, ever goes out and watches her husband fly?" I paused for breath. "The answer is no one. I mean no one. I'll tell you that." He had made the accusation before on more than one occasion and I had thought about it. I was thinking of Bob Caterson of Bob Caterson Buicks selling used cars in Indianapolis when I was in med school. Pointing his finger from out the TV screen: No One, No One, could sell you a used car cheaper than Bob Caterson. I finished it. "I've watched you fly every plane you've been assigned to. You don't even remember." It seemed that was the truth, he didn't remember. "When you were in pilot training, you used to turn on a headlamp when you were doing touch-and-go's just so I would know which plane you were in, and when you were in F-4 training I always came early to pick you up just to watch you come in" Every base we were stationed on had been the same with alley-sized hot cement streets that led to the flight line. I had driven them all. It was a well-kept military secret: something breath-taking in a full field of airplanes if you could find your way through that tiny maze of streets. He and I agreed on that and he knew it. "I did it all the time in B-52 training too," I said." I used to take Kelly with me and go out on the mound to the side of the base and watch. Maybe you didn't even know it sometimes. Don't you remember?" The truth was I found his forgetting more than disconcerting.

Now I could feel the constriction in my throat, thinking we might never make it out of the Air Force, much as we both loved his flying. It seemed there should be more to life than flying airplanes forever for Bryan and more for me than trailing him around from base to base.

Aloud, I said I could go to graduate school myself elsewhere. My voice was strident. "We don't really have to stay in California," I contended thinking we could both be willing to leave for each other.

Nevertheless, for all of our talk, we couldn't seem to decide anything. I started graduate school, and however it happened, Bryan began work at Beale Air Force Base.   He started as the information officer, his hope being one day, he said, to fly the SR-71. As a family we were given a tour of the base and allowed to watch a take-off and a landing, Bryan commenting that in the air the SR-71 glowed orange from the heat of the titanium from which it was constructed; it became so hot that it was malleable, this totally titanium aircraft, at mach one, the speed of sound. They referred to it as the blackbird.

We both were relieved to be assuming some routine of living. Bryan gave Rotary and Lions Club talks and Chambers of Commerce talks about the SR-71 with enthusiasm, looking forward to flying the SR-71 himself before long. I was, at last, glad to be back in science.

Between us, we were commuting well over 150 miles a day: he, north to Marysville, where the SR-71's were stationed, and I, west to Davis, on the diagonal road toward the Pacific Ocean, from Sacramento down to San Francisco. The freeway from my side of Sacramento, bordering on the hills going up to Lake Tahoe, was completed the fall I started. It was easy access back to graduate school, I thought.

The following summer Bryan went to Squadron Officers' School, for three months in Alabama. He told me that as an exercise everyone had to fill out an application for graduate school at the Air Force Institute of Technology, in Dayton, Ohio.

I said, "Why don't you send it in?"

He said, "I already did. It takes months, sometimes over a year, to be accepted. I can decide then."

 Three weeks later he was accepted for the fall term.

Again, I said, "I guess you should go, if it's that hard to get in. You've been talking about going to grad school in physics forever."

"But how would we work it?" He already knew the answer.

"I'm not quitting this time," I said. "You go, and I'll stay until I'm finished."

"But that'll be weird," was his comment.

"So, what else is new?" I asked. I meant it. "I just can't quit this time. This is it for me. If I don't do it now, I won't do it ever. I've had enough of staying home." I pulled on his arm. "Just go. We can commute. You can take the roll-top desk and your chair and find an apartment. It'll be OK."

So we did it. I finished my degree with enough of a rough draft to write a final version elsewhere, and moved to Dayton. Bryan, back in school, was in his element. He had bought more books than he ever had as an undergraduate, discounting them on our taxes as professional supplies, and had a large bookcase-full within months. He sat in his chair, as he had a few years before, reading math books as he had then as though they were novels. It was all familiar. I moved into the apartment, and Kelly slept in the walk-in closet. She was in fourth grade, too big to be sleeping that way; we needed to find a house. I went looking and found a house, 130 years old that had been transplanted from another town to within a block from the school that Kelly had already started.

I liked the upstairs the best. Ten rooms altogether with four of them upstairs: four boxy rooms, one per wall, with steps coming up the middle: three bedrooms and a TV room which had a beige shag rug, close to ankle-deep and thick as any I had ever seen. The sliding glass doors in the TV room opened onto the roof. Bryan's big old chair and ottoman sank into the carpet on the wall opposite the glass doors onto the roof. It was one step down into the TV room from identical doors into bedrooms on either side of the chair. Often we would both sit in the chair and look out onto that roof at the sky, monitoring the midwestern weather. It seemed a new phenomenon, we had been in California for so long. We had forgotten how the weather could, and did change, precipitously.

Back of the wall behind Bryan's chair and between the two bedrooms was a giant closet. You could go between the bedrooms through the closet, by-passing the TV room, and Bryan and I plus Kelly and our German shepherds played hide-and-seek round and round the upstairs rooms, each bigger than in any apartment or house that we had stayed in: certainly bigger than the closet she had been sleeping in. We had a regular life for awhile.

Systematically, we ate out at every restaurant in Dayton that seemed appealing. For the first time we had the money to do it: a regular became a place called the Stockades, the closest easiest in-and-out restaurant for a good meal. We ate there often on week-nights. A steak and shrimp place, it was down the hill from the Air Force Museum, which was down the hill, in turn, from our house. The Air Force museum was a place we also visited regularly, with or without guests in town; it was as monstrous as any astrodome, filled with more airplanes of venerable bearing than any museum in the country. All of the U.S. Air Wars were represented: World War I, World War II, Korea, and Vietnam. In a small hall, the early Mercury space capsules were lined up in a display. And on display as well, was the first plane of bird-like fragility in appearance, flown by the Wright Brothers and singular among the Air Force array of prop and jet planes, in being constructed from wood. This town was the home of Wilbur and Orville Wright. They had owned a bicycle shop in Fairborn, the suburb now overtaken by the base where we had bought a house. This museum had grown up around the legend of the Wright Brothers.

We ate one night at another place called the Peasant Stock. We were there to see a friend of a friend, Brad Reynolds, a classical guitarist, who was then playing weekends at the Peasant Stock. He had been at our house the night before for dinner with another mutual friend and had invited us all to come the following night for dinner, should we care to hear him play. Monica who played enough classical guitar to be able to talk with Brad, had gotten out her own guitar and the two of them had taken their talk of scales, chords, technique, and guitarists they had seen in person, into my junk room under the steps. We could hear one play, and then the other, back and forth, while the rest of us sat with coffee in the dining room.

Bryan looked across the table at me quizzically. I wondered what was on his mind. He answered my thought with a question: "I didn't know Monica played the guitar so well — where did she ever learn?" he asked me directly.

"In school," I said, trying to remember myself. "She started in high school.   In college, she actually studied with some guy from India who had studied with Ravi Shankar himself."

"How come she doesn't play now?" He was still curious.

"How should I know?" I answered. "My cousin played the violin well enough to spend a summer at Interlocken, and her husband 20 years later when I kidded her about it, stated that he never even knew she had played the violin." I wondered at the sound of my voice. I had not thought I was irritable this evening. My present thought was that Bryan had a way of telling everyone what they should do with their lives. He had spent a whole evening when we lived in California telling Monica she should get a job at Disneyland, doing what none of us knew what.   It had started as a joke, but as the evening wore on, it was clear he meant it. It was also clear that Monica without a job at the time, did not find it humorous and did not have Disneyland on her mind as a possibility. We humored Bryan, as we had before, listening to him because we all knew Disneyland was the place he was talking about for himself.   It was his favorite place in California, perhaps his favorite place in the world. His love of it was his own mystery.   No one he knew would be surprised if, instead of going to work for an airline or aerospace company upon getting out of the Air Force, Bryan were to go to work at Disneyland.   Doing what would be irrelevant.

At the Peasant Stock for dinner there were just Bryan and I, even though the night before when we had all talked about it, we had all planned to come. We listened to Brad playing, and I was still thinking of the conversation of the evening before.

We ordered and I asked him, imagining Monica at Disneyland, "So, what would you do if you had your absolute choice of something different to do now?" I pictured him with Monica, in Disneyland as I said it.

He answered me without hesitation. "I'd go back to flying fighters." In finishing his Master's Degree in math at the Air Force Institute of Technology, he had been asked if he would like to continue on a Ph.D.

"But what about physics?"

"Well, what about it?"

"Isn't there anything in physics, since you're studying it now, that you would really want to study? Would you really go back to flying instead if you had a choice?"

He answered, not unsurprisingly, "I would always go back to flying." He went on, "If I had to do something academic, and if I could wave a wand for what I would want to figure out, it would be a general theory of relativity."

"So, what stops you from pursuing that?"

"It's not enough of a challenge."

I said, slowly, "You mean, maybe it's too much of challenge." I looked straight at him over the candlelight. Brad was still playing in the background and our voices hadn't yet gotten unacceptably loud for being in a restaurant. I pressed on. "Like maybe it's too much of a risk. You might have to get out of the Air Force and go be a real academic."

He leaned forward. I wondered if his chin would get singed by the candle between us. "There is no big risk in being a physicist. Those guys live in a literal ivory tower. The only real risk in this life is physical risk. I'm in much more danger hanging off the side of a mountain or hanging upside down in an airplane pulling six g's than sitting at my desk thinking physics."

We were now in the middle of a conversation we'd had in pieces before. It was congealing. "I suppose that's one way to look at it. You won't die at your desk. You're saying the only real risk, then, is physical risk?"

I waited for him to answer me with 'Roger that'. A flying expression I had come to hate.

"There is no risk except physical risk. There is no such thing as mental risk." He was reiterating his point all right. We both knew I did not mountain climb and I didn't know how to fly. I couldn't talk about both and he could, but he was leaving it subtly unsaid.

I said it nevertheless, "Well, I beg to differ." My voice was still calm. "My guess is that for you who knows it all, going out there into the real world to be a hot-shot physicist is one order of magnitude more intimidating to you than screwing up in the air or sliding off the side of some mountain. At the least, it's not negligible on the risk-scale."

I went on. "And while we're at it, if that's what it is for you, how come, after all these years, you haven't been climbing once? Since we've been married, I mean. And how come you don't have your private pilot's license, so you can at least go out and tottle around? You were the one who said, all it would take is taking a test and a couple of rides. I mean you do have a multi-engine license, right. You complain about never flying anymore. I saw your license in a drawer someplace. You could fly an airliner tomorrow."

I was going on and on. "The thing is, we, neither of us, does anything. Not anything we talk about. Together or separately."

He broke in, "You never could decide what the hell you did want to do." He had a point. "I mean I've asked and asked what do you want to do, where do you want to live? You never know. At least I'm doing something."

"Sure, you work. So do I. You think I should be selling drugs for some pharmaceutical company. You don't want to hear about doing real science. I mean we could live Air Force-style, in Albuquerque, New Mexico or Dayton, Ohio, some choices. Whatever happened to the rest of it? I thought you were going to be Lawrence of Arabia?"

"We got married." He was looking straight at me.

"We sure did." I looked back, wondering how it was that enough was never enough from each other.

We needed, I thought, to be something more. Separately and together. It wasn't the thing of doing itself, so I thought, but what hopefully, it would do to ones' lives. So I told myself. Change life into something less than mundane, more than this. Give it a purpose. I thought of Will and Ariel Durant, spending their lives writing the history of the world together. That had to be better than this. Doing nothing. Barbecuing on the week-ends.

"You know," I said, "You say, you never say anything bad about me. The worst you could tell the NASA shrink was that I don't screw the lids on jars down tight. You say you pick them up and the bottoms fall off. Peanut butter on the floor. Well, that's crap. You're saying that's all that's wrong with me. The jars do fall, that's a fact. To me, never mind everyone one else you brag to, you never say anything positive. Only in public. You tell me what I read is boring. You read Fitzgerald and then tell me he's boring, just as you knew he would be to prove your point. You tell me jazz is boring, and you put on Johnny Cash singing about The Man in Black as though his prancing around Folsom Prison in a cowboy outfit and mask will blotto the images of my favorite piano-players, as you like to call them."

Our errantry, when it came to mutual expectations, was also mutual. One would have to be a magician physically and mentally, or be both, in order to exact each from him-self or herself, what would satisfy the other. Maybe our oddity of my being tall and his being short set us off on a chase that was to be both mental and physical and would also be endless. The best for us would have been to come out the same size in the first place: the wizardry was not now possible. This had started some years before. The day that I had met Bryan in a summer lab job, I asked him what his undergraduate major was. He had answered, "Biology."

I had smiled to myself. "Do you want to go to med school?" I asked. He was between his sophomore and junior years in college then, nineteen going on twenty that summer.

"How did you know?" he in turn, asked of me. I could see how surprised he was. "I'd like to live all over the world, and I figure being an M.D.is the best and easiest way to do it."

"Really," I said. I who had fancied myself at sixteen as a female Albert Schweitzer practicing medicine and pre-serving life — taking care not even to step on ants — in the

African wilderness, had never thought of medicine as a means to travel the world, and my med school buddies as far as I knew all just wanted to graduate and complete a residency in order to set up practice in a permanent environs. It was my turn to register surprise.

He went on to explain by saying he had met a French family in Lebanon in which the father was an M.D. who had traveled practicing medicine in just that way, all over the world. Bryan had met them on a visit to their home with his father who was in the Foreign Aid Service at the time. There were seven children in the family. Clearly the mother must have been both efficient and exotic.

Sitting there, now at the Peasant Stock we were paying little attention to Brad's classical guitar that we had come to hear. Even then, little did we know about the coming cataclysm. One would think the portent would be there, in some collective momentum of the tables' decorative candles: some unison in their flickering. I was thinking about my evaluation of all his former girl friends. Maybe one of them would have made the perfect Lebanese Model of the Happy Housewife. Petit and Pretty. He had actually tried to persuade me more than once to wear bright red lipstick. I did it one time. Later, feeling ghoulishly clown-like, I had said. "I'm a redhead. That's enough color. Just buzz off." It was, it seems, that we each asked of one another more than one person can be at once and still be one person. What did I ask that was unreasonable? Only that in his off hours of flying he be — *an artiste* — I would secretly half-think and half-wish to myself, with enough insanity to write poetry, but not too much to keep him from flying or from being the astronaut he had told me he wanted to be. He was, in fact, my hero. I just wanted more.

I had now a feeling of mutual stymie. Perhaps one could say we were stalling out. Not funny perhaps. "Can you deny it?" That part of my thought came out aloud while I was staring. Bryan looked at me across the table. I tried to refocus on him.

"Deny what?"

"That we're at the end of our rope?" There wasn't a

physical image that didn't fit. Flying or climbing. In Switzerland, at sixteen, he had fallen off the Jungfrau. He said the guide had watched him reel out about l000 yards. Now that the conversation had taken this turn, I knew he would probably find that less hazardous than this. But physical hazard was not the question for him. It was the source of the basic disagreement between us. He would smile, then, and ask, what was my problem. If I were a believer in mental versus physical risks, what was my reason for being in the arm chair myself? He could say he was bored, and that was that. In a minute, he would get up and go do aerobatics down the road someplace at a local airport. My excuses were poor. It was just easier to turn it back on him.

"Don't you want more" I asked.

He said no. "Flying is all there is."

The preceding few weeks Bryan had spent getting ready to go to a NASA interview. This week, he had just gotten back. Bob, his best friend and now an oral surgeon, had filled his cavities. Bryan had bought a weight-lifting set-up. He straight out quit smoking for the week. This was l978, the year that a general solicitation was sent out by NASA. Nationwide on bulletin boards from the post office to university physical and biological science departments, there were the announcements. I had seen them and wondered if Bryan wouldn't want to apply. NASA was actively recruiting astronauts. He had already started his application. I don't even remember seeing the application, nor his talking about sending it in. I heard more about it on national news from time to time in the evenings. The first thing I remember was his saying he was going for an interview, in about ten days. This time I hadn't even seen an application on the dining room table.

"Great," I said. I was truly smiling.

Two hundred of 6000 or so applicants were to be interviewed, in two groups, l00 at a time. He knew he had a good chance. Combat flying had given him, and those like him, more hours than anyone could compete with. It was one plus. Another was his memory. He came back from the interview saying he had repeated numbers until the interviewer tired of listening to him. And there was his physical stamina. He had, in fact, in the turning Barone chair, used by neurologists to check the inner ear canals, lasted according to the swirler that day, longer than anyone he had ever seen. Bryan had always seemed immune from becoming dizzy.

He said that the psychiatrist stated that every astronaut candidate, with the exception of the civilians who had no flying training, and with no exception concerning pilots, would choose, when questioned, to do whiffordils in the sky, that was the phrase, as opposed to some kind of constructive activity.

We stared at each other now. His last comment was a compound sentence the second half of which was completed by his look. He did not have to say that he was vindicated. We were both thinking of his NASA interview. Physical risk would henceforth take the day over mental risk in any argument we could have, from his standpoint, with impunity. NASA had vindicated him. The conclusion of the conversation at the Peasant Stock stood. I had after all, commended him for his astronaut aspirations from the beginning, the drugstore stool days. If I didn't like the selection procedure, natural or otherwise, I could lump it. It was real. They were all of a group.

In another week I came back from my graduation from UC Davis. Bryan had not gone. I was surprised that I had. It was, in fact, more meaningful than I had expected. It was a relatively small ceremony and 108 in Davis-degrees. A typical Northern California summer. I marched in last without my advisor who was serving as marshall of the ceremonies. My own parents and Kelly were there watching with the others.

Back in Dayton, the next week I found Bryan sitting in his chair every evening before dinner, drinking a small glass of sherry. We did not eat at the Stockades that week and Friday night I sat myself on the monstrous footstool and looked at him, the fingers of both hands braced in their interlacings over my knees. But I was not prepared.

He swallowed like he did when he had given SR-71 speeches about melting titanium and said slowly that we were going to have to get a divorce. We had never mentioned the word before. Nevertheless, our minds had gone full circle simultaneously. Each day I had wondered if I could stand one day more of what had turned into a stony silence between us. He apparently had been wondering the same.

"I know," I said. "Whatever are we going to do?"

"Get a divorce, that's all. I feel subhuman."

I felt the shock of his words. He had been as distraught as I, and I hadn't noticed. Had he not seen it in me? Or had he? I had thought he was just not thinking, period. I'd had to think that. Instead we had been thinking in exact parallel.

He didn't know I had been telling myself every day that I had to pack a bag and get away from him. It was more than the metal gun box, crate-sized, to house all of the guns, the machine-gun included, that he was collecting. I didn't understand, but a house-full of guns was mild compared to the rest, if I could find a way to stand the rest. It remained nebulous. I couldn't even find it to stand it.

He went on. "I should never have come back. I wish I hadn't made it."

I lay back on the stool, my head and feet hanging over the sides and I stared at the ceiling. The late afternoon sun was like flat latex paint — yellow on the painted-white ceiling. "You shouldn't say that," I said. There were tears inching up into my hair, on my upside down head, dangling off of the footstool. I sat up and they reversed direction down behind my shirt collar. He knew better, or did he. It wasn't a question of whether we cared about one another or not: what we were learning was that we couldn't live together now. We had never done it for any time at all before. We were not practiced. And it had to do with more than his going to sleep regularly when the sun rose and I was waking. It had more to do with two people expecting from each other what is humanly impossible than it had to do with sleeping and rising in alteration. In some far-recess, it had to do with more even than that. There was in the moment before I sat upright again on the footstool, an awful dawn of thought. He had told me twice in his life that he would die at 28, once the summer I met him when he was nineteen turning twenty, sitting in a tree spotting squirrels, and once in the December that he was shot down.

I closed my eyes to the face of the ceiling. Beyond our own defect there was another, one of a second order: a stepped-up chemical reaction. This defect was incurred. I couldn't believe what he had just said. But I knew what he meant. It was that we had both survived the war and the others, John and Michael, and because of them, Ellen and Renee, their children and their families, had not.

And in our recoil from each other, we were about to compound our guilt. The Ship's Captain, John Paul Jones, held the day: we were criminals, he and I, in our survival. Bryan, who had knowingly flown in the series of the heaviest nights of bombing in the history of aerial warfare, most likely the heaviest night in all of history and for an ambiguous cause, was guilty for not having gone down with his ship; after giving the order for everyone to eject and on the chance that someone would be killed in the SAM attacks on their B-52, he would live with the thought that he should have gone down with it. No matter what. I lay back and said nothing. The realization that he should live with such a thought was, second to Colleen's death, the most appalling I had ever had.

Now, it was late in our lives. There seemed no place to go, except oppositely, away from each other, if we were to survive. We filled up the room too fast together with our travail. We could not look at each other. I asked him some days later if he would go back to California and see the POW psychiatrist I had learned to like in the wives' group.

"No," he said, "No way." I didn't have what it took to insist.

"Why not?" My question was half-hearted.

"Just because," was all he said. We, both of us, hadn't the hope for any of it.

18

AFTER VIETNAM

ONE

Upstairs, the sun filled the bedroom - seeming so bright and heavy you could almost have thought it had pushed the window sills to the floor. In fact, the house was 130 years old and had been built this way, with windows as tall as the rooms were high. They were at least ten feet tall, with tops and bottoms barely inches from floor and ceiling. When I lay on my bed, the window sill, if I wanted to set a glass on it, was a foot below my bed level, and I sometimes imagined that I was in a tree house.

Lying on the bed for once simultaneously these days, Bryan and I were having a scientific discussion of sorts. He had just returned from the Air Force Academy where a friend of a friend was working on an X-ray analysis of a cloth purported to be from the body of Jesus, taken after the Crucifixion. The Shroud of Turin. I had never heard of it. Bryan was sounding fanatical about it. I looked at him as I had at times in the past, not quite understanding. In one moment he could turn from the greatest of atheists into a weird True Believer: I had never settled on either in my mind about him.

He had spread on the bed, a book in paper back, <u>The Shroud of Turin: A Scientific Inquiry</u>, and a number of scientific papers concerning the subject, all which he had just hauled out of his briefcase. He was now telling me that this shroud, as he showed me from one colored plate in the book, was of a pale maize-colored cloth, and he related to me that it carried an image of the body of Jesus somehow imprinted upon it.

This imprint was made supposedly at the time the body lay in the sepulchre following its removal from the cross. The book contained not only photographic plates of the shroud as it is today, and photos of the places it has been retained during its history, but it also contained 3-D image analyzer tracings, which this Air Force friend of a friend, another Air Force captain stationed at the Academy and doing this on the side, was involved in making: X-ray films, diagrams, and photos of microscopic enlargements of special squared-off areas of the shroud, of blood stains, even of insect parts found in it, and of separated fibrils, preserved in their disintegration from the shroud proper.

All of it was done in the interest of examining the question of the Turin Shroud's authenticity.

Many authorities called it an artistic forgery. If now known to be a fake, to me calling it an artistic forgery seemed an awkward designation for it. I would have thought that an artistic forgery, *per se*, would relate to some item that was intended as an object of art in the first place, the forgery being simply a copy of it. Hardly the case with the Turin Shroud.

The thing that seemed to be overwhelming Bryan was that this photo of the shroud, consisting of a dark outline of a head and body, having arms crossed from the perspective of a prone position, over the abdomen, was less clear than a photo of the photographic negative itself.

The photo of the negative looked more like a regular picture of it in terms of the casting of dark and light over the facial contours: the cheek bones, eye sockets, mouth shape, and skull outline, were clearer. All of these aspects in the photo itself were fuzzy. I was having a hard time concentrating.

The point that he was trying to make was that a body imprint appeared to have been transferred to the shroud in an anomalous manner. According to Bryan's Air Force Academy acquaintance, it might have been an electromagnetic transferral. That could explain the appearance of photographs as negative, rather than positive images, of the imprinted body of Jesus.

"Come on now," I said, getting interested, "How can that work?" We were propped up on opposite elbows on the bed facing each other at this point.

"Well, remember a negative of a film is reversed from the actual object. If the right hand were crossed over the left, and a normal imprint were made by the body on the shroud, then in a photo the right hand would appear to be crossed over the left as on the body. But if the imprint itself came out like a photographic negative, by some weird means of transferral, something electromagnetic, then in a photo, the left hand would appear to be crossed over the right."

I lay back on the bed and crossed my hands, right over left, imagining the cloth material over me and how it would appear if my body left behind some kind of damp marking imprint upon it. Bryan crouched on the bed, while I crossed and uncrossed my hands and I imagined seeing the cloth from the top first like it had made a regular straight up imprint, and then seeing it as a photographic negative, sides reversed.

"Then what happens when you take a picture?"

"It all goes through a reversal stage, in the negative, then back to normal in the positive; that's the photo."

We tried it both ways on each other: I crossed his right hand over his left, for a normal imprint; his left hand over his right, for the weird inexplicable imprint. Bryan had had it all on his mind for the two days of his trip; besides, it wasn't hard anyway. But still I was getting tired. I lifted the top of his crossed hands and punched his stomach with it. His contortions of doubling up were exaggerated while I jumped off the bed to avoid getting punched back, and then we tried it again: this time with imagining a coin over a closed eye, on just one eyelid.

A slit-like white line distinguished the coinless eyelid from the other in the photo: the placing of coins over the closed eyes of the dead was a practice developed in those times, and there was a whole chapter in the book devoted to the type of coins extant during that period, as further evidence of the shroud's authenticity. The data were also presented as evidence for placing of the shroud itself in the context of time that Jesus was to have lived.

We both went through the mental steps of the coin

on the eyelid: covering one of our respective eyes with one hand - easier than the crossed hands thing - the making of an imprint, the photographic negative and the photographic positive, of both regular and irregular kinds of imprints of the body of Jesus on the Turin Shroud.

TWO

Downstairs, he sat at the dining room table, with all of his Dungeons and Dragons paraphernalia laid out, late into the night, rolling dice to determine his character's character for this game to be played around this huge oval with his group of buddies that night. They were a mixture of Air Force people, stationed at Wright Patterson Air Force Base and of my lab friends whom he'd come to know. Also coming was the owner of the store, way on the south side of town, from whom he'd bought the game.

It was from this town of Dayton, Ohio, this north side of Dayton even, that some young man at Michigan State University who played it in the flesh in the university's steam tunnels, had died mysteriously during the playing of it in these tunnels. A few years after the game playing of Bryan and his friends had waned, I saw a photo of Bryan, dressed like a weird-hooded warrior from ancient history, and it was then that I thought of this young college man and his family. Later, I learned Bryan's garb was authentic; he was dressed like a seafaring Viking and the horns on his head, therefore, were not of his own imagination. They could, in fact, be viewed in the Encyclopedia Britannica. But the learning was too late for me, and I blamed the state of my life at that time on the game of Dungeons and Dragons.

Now it was 3:00 in the morning. I wasn't certain what had wakened me, sleeping downstairs in my small yellow room where I seemed to be spending my evening and week-end hours, some all-nighters, typing my Ph.D. thesis. I was trying the meet the December deadline at the University of California, now light years away. It was a tiny room, off the dining room of this relic of a house; the house itself made me think of a description of Freud's home in Vienna, due to its front room being separated from the dining room by a door three inches thick, too heavy to move without both of us to pull it. There in Freud's home, a room like this was an office for patients at the front of the house, with the family living quarters at the back: here in Ohio, this front room, set a little bit to the side, had been a barber shop.

I had liked the house I decided later, for two reasons, this barber shop aspect being one, and its location just one block from an actual old-fashioned dime store, called Foy's, being the other. In Foy's, everything was stacked up high in the corners and on the counters; items were laid out in the open in compartments made of cardboard, simply divided, depending upon the size of the item. These were filled with everything from sequins to nails. In the fall, Indian Summertime, windows were hung with rubber masks on clothesline strings for Halloween. Kelly and her friends made a haunted house in the basement just to have an excuse to go buy masks from Foy's.

Bryan and I had agreed on both houses, in California and in Ohio, almost sight unseen, saying to both realtor ladies, "This one will do," just in the passing by. In Sacramento, coming down a lane of olive trees, the *For Sale* sign was out in front with no sign from the distance of an accompanying house behind, except for a gray mailbox leaning against one in a row of sky-high palms jutting evenly from what had originally been an olive grove. Up close, the house sat back from the road and was a white-washed cedar house of light. We couldn't get in to see it then, and we said it didn't matter. Together, peering over the six foot side and backyard fence and looking in the windows was enough. It would be fine. Later, we looked at it briefly and bought it.

This Ohio house was its complete opposite: in California - an unencumbered gray clapboard in an olive grove where the pale lemon-colored walls tilted in deference to the California earthquake tremors - supplanted in Ohio by: 130 years of ornate woodworking, ten foot ceilings, too many rooms to keep counted, and a dirt-floored basement with a furnace that looked and sounded like a Star Wars monster. It was balanced precariously on a cement city block of the Midwest, physically moved years prior from one town to another to preserve it historically for the state of Ohio.

In Ohio, while our life was beginning to fall apart badly and we both knew it, we repeated our house buying ritual. We hunted down with less than our usual disinterest, the familiarity of lawns and driveways, porches, and rooms to sleep and eat, perhaps to contain disquietude we didn't discuss. I made my rounds with realtors, found a house, looked in the windows, and said once more that we didn't really need to see the inside. We looked at it and bought it the next day and told our parents that we had bought a house in Ohio, visibly allaying whatever remaining doubts they had about our living together again. We looked to them for passing reassurances back to us in talk about house findings and furnishings; to date, we had been married five years and had spent less than half of that time together. And now we would be living together full-time for the first time in our marriage without the war as a regular part of it.

My favorite small room where I was finishing my thesis was under the steps to the second story. It had a thick shag rug, ankle-deep and warm even when the monster furnace failed. There were three frosted windows in a row on the outside wall, seven feet tall, but with barely inches between the wooden frames. The loosely fitted panes would clink if one moved too close or breathed too hard on the winter glass. We had an old TV in a shelved hole under the stairwell, Bryan's single bed from his mother's in one corner, and kitty-corner from it, I had my old desk. Purchased in medical school at a Goodwill Store, I assumed it had been someone else's dining room table; the leaves for it were missing when I bought it, and now there were some numbers of holes spaced on its edges and midseam for Bryan's shell reloading equipment. The room itself was so small that there was no space in the diagonal between the bed and the desk. Kelly and the neighborhood kids jumped the spot where desk and bed met, or settled for jumping on the bed by the hour: a more likely accommodation during my thesis distractions. The room, Bryan said, was too small for him.

Now at 3 AM, the cavernous place was silent and dark, with the exception of the lit chandelier over the table in the dining room and the muted sound of dice rolling on its surface. "Don't you," I said, leaning both elbows on this huge dining room table that the next night would be circled with players of the game I came to hate, "Ever feel haunted by life?"

Bryan, turning towards me owl-like without blinking from out of the shadows, looked bored instantly. Doubtless, he was suspicious of my dragging him once more, I'm sure he would say, into a maudlin conversation. But I was determined this time to make it stick. I thought of it that way. I thought of those spiders kids throw against the wall and that then walk down it, in bouts of sticking and loosing of spindly legs, moving like a real spider, but made of rubber.

I had thought about this ahead of time, even though I couldn't remember what had wakened me, certainly not the sound of rolling dice of a Dungeons and Dragons character, nor could I remember what had brought me to standing by the dining room table at 3 AM.

I hoped that I looked like an apparition and that my sudden appearance had occurred like one. It was a possibility. Bryan had a tendency to start looking bored when he was most likely to be uncomfortable about something.

Tonight I was fortified. I had found, this very day, in the one-room Fairborn library, not unlike the dimestore down the street, in its basis for my buying a house in Fairborn, a poem I had been looking for for 25 years, having seen it once and lost it. It was by Matthew Arnold, and I would have difficulty even now finding or naming it again. Then it disappeared as quickly as it had come again into the chaos of my life.

The poem's speaker was standing at a window looking

out onto a cobblestone square of an English village. The streets were darkened, and in deepening moonlight, his eyes were following the sound of hollow footsteps through the square. No person was visible with the footsteps. This book was still lying by my bed upstairs, so I could get it and read it to him if necessary. I repeated my question. "Don't you ever feel haunted by the oddness of life?"

His look asked me, surprisingly, to go on. I looked at the front door and walked to it, pressing my nose on the half-glass of that old door. "It is Kelly going to school - some days I could just weep when I watch her. I cry for letting the lamb to slaughter. But then sometimes I know she'll have the world by the tail, and I can't wait for it to happen. It is always the bittersweet. Don't you know?"

We had never gotten it straight, he and I. I had to know, finally, if he knew me.

"There is more," I said. "It is not really about Kelly at all. One night I went into the University of Dayton library to xerox an article. The lights were out, but I barely noticed the library had supposedly been locked until I realized the xerox machine was also off. Don't ask me why, but I walked to the card file, and looked up a book I've all my life meant to check in a library; the name of it is Alms for Oblivion — a book, the title of which I never knew if I made up or saw somewhere. It was in the file, a critical essay text by an English professor at the University of Minnesota; surprised, I went up and found it on the third floor of the library. There were no lights on anywhere, and it was hard to see in the stacks, but there was enough light to find the aisle and the book. It was on a top shelf." I had yet to be able to define the thing I was trying to say, but I went on.

"It was a skinny gold book with an engraving of a thin black tree with extremely narrow limbs on the gold cover. It wasn't the book, except for the title, that I had always known. I didn't recognize it, except for the title; I read it later, and strangely I found I understood very little of it. The contents were as unfamiliar as the title was familiar: the discussions were of the writing styles of various authors, some of whom I didn't even recognize. Perhaps I wasn't well enough read even for the authors I knew. But it doesn't matter. If it is not about Kelly, it is about that: Alms for Oblivion. I know that I would go begging, upon certain occasions, for oblivion."

Now was not the time. I knew that. Our conversations were sporadic at best these days. Talking bittersweet was beyond us for sure. I went into the family room, an added-on room, since the 130 years' inception; it was a room that made no sense, the blasted house was already monstrous in size. There were some ten or fifteen rooms. The huge brick fireplace was all this room had going for it, the family room that is, and it was plenty ugly even so, constructed of an odd sort of beige brick. I grabbed my recording of Mendelssohn's Violin Concerto, his one and only, and said through the door, "If you want to know what I'm talking about, this says it OK." I put it on the stereo and watched the needle slip and whir across the whole disk.

The whole situation was dumb. We were 36 and 39 years old. At 18 and in my father's house, he'd put on Madame Butterfly for me and smiled (leered?) at me. Not now. I headed upstairs, those narrow, steep steps, many of them, to my rambling second floor, hand on the banister in the dark. I was wondering what the hell I was doing up. I heard Mendelssohn begin, those violins, that one violin, "I'll tell you about absolution some time if you like." I started back downstairs. Bryan was on his way up, and we crossed at the bottom.

"What you want," he said, and I could hear the derision in his voice, "is a soul-mate."

"Yeah, so what.?" I said. I was apologetic nevertheless. "So what do you want?" What he meant, we both knew, was I was too old, 39 years, to still be wanting such. I should have grown up by now. He had a point. So why did his face seem to be dissembling before me in the dark. I could feel it if I couldn't see it, the flesh running into the night shadows.

We both stood at the base of the stairs, one foot on the bottom step (ready to leap?), each of us, opposite hands on opposite rails of those plush carpeted steps, steep enough to be ladder-steps or attic-steps. The dark up there wasn't dark enough to hide him or me.

I did know him, exactly what he would look like if someone flicked on the lights. The distortion of his face, probably related to the pull of the old, what should stay in the past, he would say. Madame Butterfly was, and should be, long gone. A mental asterisk to our past. Now, who could make it up the steps the fastest was the real question. Always the dare by the one and the counted on response by the other.

"I just want someone to have fun with." I heard him say it.

"Yes, I know," I heard and saw myself, from lots of angles. I knew I was no longer any fun. "The bottom line in that book, Alms for Oblivion," I said, "If you want to know, is absolution from anguish. That's it."

I headed up the steps to my bed where I lay back and opened the black-on-gold book from the library that I couldn't read; I lay the opened book across my chest, face-down, my fingers intertwined over my rib cage, and closed my eyes, relieved that after all these years, I had found it at last.

THREE

The Domestic Relations Court of the city of Dayton, Ohio, is located in the basement of one of those numerous limestone city-county buildings found in midwestern cities. Before I had even moved to Dayton, I had paired it as a city with Detroit itself, in competing for being the toughest city in the Midwest: places uneasy to be in even for a native of these middle states. Detroit and Dayton were sore thumb protrusions taking their places with New York, Chicago, Boston, and LA, as major crime-ridden cities on the U.S. map.

We'd had a flat tire on the periphery of Dayton's inner city, the very first day we were there, and I could see even Bryan lose his bravado and become relieved to get one tire off and another on. Weeks later I learned to go downtown

alone, wary as I was of doing it because of all I'd heard
both inside and outside the Midwest itself. I was taking
Kelly, whose fourth grade aspiration was to be a ballerina,
to lessons at the Dayton Ballet Company, located on the
corner of Main and First. The studio was on the second
floor of an edifice just about to crumble and just a block
from the site of our flat tire. The first time Kelly and I were
on our way to a ballet lesson, hand in hand, a tall somber
man had jumped from a stairwell telling me guilefully that
I was beautiful; Kelly pulled on my hand and we hurried on.
Minutes later a reporter, carrying a TV camera, halted us
head-on at a street corner, startling me all the more, to ask
if I would care to speak on the Afghanistan invasion, and
saying no thank you, we hurried on again.

Nevertheless, after a few trips and finding a safe path
to follow, I grew quite accustomed to going into downtown
Dayton. Kelly and I would go on each Tuesday in her fourth
grade winter, park in the lot straight across the street, and
I would either sit in the slow light of the waiting room listening to the music and the kids thumping the wooden
floors as I read magazines, or I would shop for the hour idly
in Rike's, the major downtown department store, adjacent
to the parking lot.

Every city in these midwestern states has one, perhaps
two, nice department stores as they are always referred to,
such as Marshall Field's of Chicago and Strauss' of
Indianapolis, likely to be constructed of limestone turned
blue-black with the years and edged with cornices and win-
dow-trims too ornate for a simple glance, but never receiv-
ing more. Always there is a clock, usually four-sided, on the
department store's street corner. I remember great black
numbers and hands and thin pointy arrows on the tips of
the hands on the corner clock at Strauss', on the
Indianapolis Monument Circle, too flimsy - one would
deem - for the changes in weather that would come with
the season, but their slow rotation was invariable for marking the shopping day passage.

You do not see department stores like these in western cities, and there is a darkness in the very center of all

these midwest cities you never, never, see in cities in the west: almost a curvature of the streets, downward, leading to the center, as into a tunnel, but all you ever come to is the Main St. corner, busy with pedestrian traffic, cabs and cars, dwarfed in the shadows of the buildings leaning over the intersection.

I looked for the downtown familiarities this day as I was about to go get a divorce — it was summer, late in August, the hottest part of it. 1981, fourteen and one-half years after our marriage. The midwestern familiarity of the city, glued to my bones even without the pressure of the August heat, was serving in the converse: a premonition of the untoward. Connie was doing the driving.

Since living in Dayton, Connie had come to seem like a very old friend, except that we were both adults in our thirties when we first met. Our meeting, only a year before, had followed a telephone conversation between Bryan and someone who I assumed was an Air Force acquaintance. It had started with flying. Then Bryan smiled and motioned to me to come sit with him: the conversation went to computers, guns, cars, politics, motorcycles, and finally to teeth. In its turn to teeth, I knew that it was his oldest friend Bob. They had gone to high school together in Ft. Wayne, Indiana, and then to Purdue. Bob had been our best man. He had gone to dental school when Bryan went to pilot training. And Connie, who came to seem as much like a childhood friend to me as Bob did to Bryan, had married Bob. They had just moved from Michigan where he had recently finished an oral surgery residency at the University of Michigan. Now he was setting up practice, by pure coincidence, in Dayton.

Connie and I found a place to park, walked to a tenth floor office met the man who had become my lawyer after Bryan and I had started out together with him; I was never sure whether the reason for getting his own was that he believed what he told me, that I was sneaking around behind his back somehow, or whether it was that he couldn't resist the name of the one he retained from the telephone book: Ronald MacDonald.

My lawyer and Connie and I walked the short distance from his office to the supposedly new courthouse. The ride down the elevator in his building, 18 floors, was about the length of the distance we walked to the courthouse, totally routine for him, much less than routine for Connie, and gang-plank like for me. Inside, the steps were wide and shallow. Fake marble. It all seemed an odd setting for what we saw at the bottom.

There were ten or more couples, dressed-up and lined-up at a large door, each chittering together, seemingly like any normal couple, as though they had just been asked some ridiculous question by a game show host. These were dissolutions, not divorces: couples agreeing on their own terms, with no contest involved, some without lawyers altogether. They had filled in their own forms and filed the papers themselves. Supposedly that was what we were doing, Bryan and I.

I could see the judge through the door; a raised platform was at the right end of the courtroom, the door at the back facing the last row of pew-like benches. You could see her behind a large bench in front on this raised platform. There was a railing separating the court room proper from her bench.

I looked around surreptitiously to see if Bryan had shown up yet. We were not suing each other either, for anything. Our courtroom time was 10:45 and we still had 30 minutes. Connie spotted him behind the line. Looking over, I was certain of what he was thinking. I half-expected him, between the heads of the couples, to shrug in his usual way, the understanding was better tacit with us, always, let's get-the-hell-out-of- here, and I half-expected that I would probably go.

10:45 came, and all was on time. Our names were called, and we went in and seated ourselves.

The judge started: "In the Common Pleas Court of of Montgomery County, Ohio, Division of Domestic Relations, Case Number CM-81-1298, the petitioners Layne McLean Martin and Bryan Douglas Martin, now enter into a Decree of the Dissolution of Marriage."

Little doubt about that.   We had been in the process of dissolving all we knew of adult life for some time now. The Wicked Witch of the West dissolved didn't she, on the spot. The thing was more than figurative.   Saying that we hardly needed a piece of paper to make it official, was simply to hide our mutual fears of its formalizing step. It made a difference. We had to acknowledge that it had taken us a full year after getting the papers, not contesting anything, just to get ourselves here.

"Would the petitioners please stand and come forward," the judge's voice continued. Bryan and I looked at each other across the benches that were empty except for our lawyers and for Connie, and stood up, both of us awkwardly, to go forth and participate in this odd ceremony.

I tried to think of the people I knew who were actually divorced, irritated already that no one had told me that this was like a wedding ceremony. I had detested my wedding dress, a weird dark green velvet thing Bryan dreamed up and I had made. I never knew if it came out like he expected. Today, at least, it was a relief not to be standing together in it.

In the end, the whole thing seemed very long and not a little diabolical. I knew that aspect of it would get Bryan through it, and he would know that for me it wouldn't be enough. But my advantage over him this time was my tallness, and I should stand up straight. We would both get through it.

The judge herself did not seem convivial about it. It was taking forever: the Separation Agreement and Property Settlement: each of us "hereinafter" referred to as 'wife' and as 'husband': words we'd never quite gotten around to using on each other even when joking:

ARTICLE I.   SEPARATION.
ARTICLE II.   CUSTODY.
ARTICLE III.   CHILD SUPPORT.
ARTICLE IV.   VISITATION.
ARTICLE V.   DIVISION OF PROPERTY
ARTICLE VI.   HEALTH INSURANCE

ARTICLE VII.   COMPLETE SETTLEMENT.
ARTICLE VIII.   INCORPORATION INTO DECREE.
ARTICLE IX.   IMPLEMENTATION INTO AGREEMENT.

We stood at the rail concentrating hard on looking at the judge, as though she were going to save us in this dilemma, avoiding glancing at each other altogether, when in fact the judge was just getting ready to bring our dilemma to a head.

"Are you Bryan D. Martin?"

"I am."

"And are you Layne M. Martin?"

"I am."

She inclined her head just slightly.   In what already had appeared to be a disapproving attitude, this was just another angle of it.   I thought of Michael Rossman, now a near Nobel Prize winner, who had introduced us in his lab, and who, whether due to scientific absent-mindedness or actual disapproval, I never knew which, had never acknowledged our marriage.

"You, Mr. Martin, were born July 16, 1943, in Boston, Massachusetts. Is that correct?"
"It is."
"And Layne Martin, you were born May 26, 1941, in Washington, D.C., is that not correct?"
"It is."
"You are both U.S. citizens?" Another rhetorical question. We nod.

Midway into the proceedings, she asks if the financial arrangements are satisfactory to each of us. Bryan answers yes, and my response, before I check myself to say yes, is "Fairly so."

She asks me to repeat it. "Fairly so, " I said. I could feel everyone stiffen, my own lawyer included, as he had better things to do than to get bogged down in a dissolution hearing, and he had, in fact, spent weeks trying to get me to sue in a proper divorce, to the extent of calling Bryan's lawyer, Ronald MacDonald, without telling me to say that was what I was going to do; but my feeling penniless was what Bryan said was a fair trade for my Ph.D.; I was on my own now, Baby; I chickened out and corrected myself: "The terms are acceptable."

Finally it all ended. The procedural part had taken all of approximately ten minutes. Bryan and I did not look at each other again, and Connie and I left the city hall. That afternoon I threatened to visit the father of a woman I knew was interested in Bryan already. Her father, I thought, was most interested in Bryan on her behalf. He was a retired Air Force major who belonged to the Soldier of Fortune organization; he attended Soldier of Fortune conventions and I had seen him in camouflaged clothing driving a camouflaged jeep. I understood machine guns were a particular interest of his, Bryan's having purchased a gun storage cabinet for the safekeeping of his own guns like that of the major's, what I referred to as a casket since it was a horizontal rather than a vertical item and of the size and shape of a casket. It was a six foot iron box complete with locking lid of iron. I suggested to him that perhaps he had in mind buying a machine gun to go with his casket. He noncommittally answered yes. He already had it ordered and the MAC 10 would be coming in to Tipp City any week now. It had required special dispensation, a written permit, from the local police but that was not a problem in this military suburb of Dayton: a better recommendation for machine gun purchasing could hardly be had than by an Air Force Officer. I was ready to take on the retired major. I would tell him what I thought of what I considered to be the major's plans for his daughter and of his general unseemly machine rat-a-tat-tat-gun-style, interference in my private life, never mind Bryan's similar purchase of such. I didn't like any of it, and I should have taken a stand already.

Connie begged me not to get into my car and go there.

"You may end up dead, Layne," she said. "You know what a gun freak he must be." We had discussed at length his camouflage situation. Later I remembered that he had been to my house before Bryan and I had even discussed divorce.

I stopped my pacing in Connie's living room, "I suppose you have a point." I knew it was not smart.

"There is nothing you can do about it now. Just don't go, not today."

"OK," I said. "I'll wait until tomorrow."

19

RECOMBINANT DNA

The next day I rented a U-Haul at the corner gas station, the biggest truck they had. I had already arranged for a new friend, her name was Candy, the mother of a classmate of Kelly's who lived down the street and who had been divorced some years earlier, to help me drive to Michigan where I had taken a postdoctoral position at Michigan State University. Candy had been a truck driver in the southwestern states for some years, and as a regular semi-driver, she had taken her daughter Alisha in a carrier next to her on the front seat of the cab for the time that Alisha had been a baby. She said it would be no problem driving a U-Haul to Michigan because, even without seeing it, she knew that a large U-Haul would be smaller than any truck she had driven. I signed up for the largest U-Haul, a twenty-four footer, possible.

It was getting a job that had seemed most impossible. Month by month, I had learned to hate my Ph.D. increasingly for the difficulty it gave me in finding regular work. Nothing seemed more desirable than a technician's position; I couldn't think straight enough for more than that. I had sent letters to the world, after reading scientific paper after paper, trying to catch up, trying to find a real scientific position. If I were to have a proper career in science, I needed a good postdoctoral position to start with, perhaps even two, with publications to show for them. I wrote to Genentech, then newly formed and the first biotechnology company in the country. I received a polite negative response from the Personnel Department. I would learn soon enough that getting a job occurs by scientific contacts. My advisor at UC Davis didn't know where I was now, and I had nothing to show for the time I had spent at the University of Dayton, a school no one would have heard of anyway. I wrote to a few places on the east coast, and the same thing happened. I was in scientific oblivion. Finally, in one of what I came to think of as my flash phone calls from a phone booth while at work, I called Massachusetts

General Hospital about a technical position advertised in the Boston Globe, one of the newspapers I had taken to buying week-ends at a newstand in Dayton.

Most of all, I thought I wanted to go to Boston, and I would be disappointed on Sundays, if the Globe, of all cities' papers, was sold out by the time I checked the newstand counter. The drive to the newstand weekly was like my flash phone calls to the world: a mustering of momentary lucidity in which the pure terror of taking on my own life and the thought of the consequences otherwise were the sole energy sources. The thought of a career in science seemed ludicrous: for the present, getting my teeth brushed was an accomplishment.

On the telephone with Massachusetts General Hospital, the Personnel Department, on a day toward the middle of my demise and from my phone booth, I was told that formal applications were accepted only for Masters Degree applicants and below. I waited a few days, called again in a different voice, lied about my degree, and asked for an application. I thought that I sounded normal enough. The fact was that in the lab I had recently taken to washing lab glassware in the afternoons with the undergraduates working in the lab. As in all labs, dishwashing was a job for undergraduates. My resorting to it was a result of having messed up a major experiment of my own by reversing the order of samples being monitored in a scintillation counter and then losing track of which was which when I discovered my error. On the heels of this, I worked a three day preparation of a coenzyme, as it was called, purified from rat liver, a tricky procedure itself calculated by Archibald Sanger, the professor whose lab at the University of Dayton this was, to be worth $63,000 in commercial dollars, each time we did it.

For his work, purification of the coenzyme was a necessity, a prerequisite to pursuing his real interests, the purification and characterization of glucocorticoid enzymes; his lab was an array of column chromatography equipment that consisted of glass or plexiglas apparatus looking like hollow tubes, to be packed with varieties of material for an endless series of enzyme purification steps. This prefactory coenzyme preparation itself had taxed my fleeting fits of verve to the ultimate. My scintillation counter incident in mind, I had concentrated very carefully to pull it off, double-checking all of my spectrophotometer readings, repeating all of my calculations, and working twelve hours a day those three days. It required twenty-four rat livers. One had to work fast after killing the rats. Sanger, the boss, was out of town. I sent the undergrads home evenings for the three-day prep and worked alone on it. I worked on ice, even when not necessary, in order to get the best possible yield. It had worked, I purified some milligrams of good coenzyme, and my scientific demise felt complete.

One ad in the Boston Globe that I called about was for a research position in a hospital laboratory. It was an immunology-related job, a subject about which I knew very little. But the M.D. who advertised the job, suggested in my rapid-fire telephone call, that I come for an interview. After the interview, he asked me to dinner and then took me to his house, a huge mansion on the Boston Harbor, complete with tennis courts, a library, sun room, and kitchen floors of marble. The M.D., an internist, whose wife had recently left him, told me if I would come and live with him, he wouldn't care what research I undertook in the lab. The next day he closed his office door and implored me, this man I had met yesterday, to come and take the position. His desperation was apparently worse than mine: I felt his secretary watching through the door, myself opening it then and easing out into the hall, sensing by some wordless and obscure elimination process that my missing out on life at present had to do with more than not having my house any longer. I found a taxi to the airport and in the weeks to follow, quit reading the Boston Globe for job ads.

Somehow, some weeks later, an opportunity at Michigan State University had come and I was taking it. I went for an interview, driving from Canada instead of Ohio, having spent two weeks with my friend Eleanor, who had practiced neurology until recently, and now had just completed a psychiatry residency at Cornell. On the telephone one Saturday morning, she had caught me trying to prepare a talk for a meeting when I said I couldn't get my laundry done. By that time I was living in the apartment Bryan and I had rented for the year. I was now spending my half-year in it, with Bryan in the house. Here is where my troubles with craziness had started. She asked me how far the laundry machines were from my apartment. In fact, I could see the laundry room and the pool both from my window.

Ten minutes later she called me back with an ultimatum.

"Look Layne, you've got two days to show up in Buffalo, or I'll be out to get you," she said, admonishing me that she'd have to take off from work to come get me. Then she told me to get myself into the swimming pool.

That I didn't do, but I managed to show up in the Buffalo airport two days later. She put me to bed in her own bed that night, leaning to turning the light out over me, telling me good-night and saying that tomorrow things would start getting better. I awoke thinking it was the first time I had slept in an entirety of three months. I put on my best silk blouse, a straight black skirt, and followed her through the motions of making coffee, packing her lunch and her brief case for work, as though I had some coordinate function when, in fact, I was going to work with her to see a psychiatrist friend of hers. I waited in her office while she made rounds. A resident appeared in the doorway, asking if I would mind if he smoked. Dr. Dickinson was the only doctor on the floor who allowed smoking. I said sure, checking out my ability to converse, I would have one with him if he didn't mind, and then Eleanor brought in her friend, Ho, Chief of Psychiatry.

Eleanor left the room, and I shifted uneasily in my chair. I wondered if she and he would want to put me into the hospital there. On her porch and in her swing the night before, I had thought she might be suggesting it. Each time we pushed off, listening to the swing's creaking, I had mustered and simultaneously lost, the courage to ask. Now I imagined dangling my feet over the edge of a hospital bed of a mental institution, wondering if I would feel safer or sorrier in an appropriate white hospital gown. Instead and to my surprise, Ho suggested I promise, in going back to Dayton for the actual divorce, to stay away from Bryan both before and after it. I was not to go to the house mornings to fix breakfast for Kelly when she was there, evenings to tuck her in, or anytime. If I could do that, he thought I could make it.

Driving from Buffalo through Canada to Michigan, for an interview at Michigan State, I had a feeling of nudity the whole way. I was, in fact, thinner than usual, but looking to the side- and rear-view mirrors, I could see that I was fully clothed. Certain that the plastic of the seats was sticking to my skin as I drove, I checked with one hand free, repeatedly for the feel of my jeans and shirt; I was not bare-boned. I drove, oblivious to the interstate traffic, in a state of envy of every pair of people I saw, pairs and pairs of them — ballooned to larger than life-sized in their cars, in rest parks and gas stations, in McDonald's. The world was squeezing me out its cracks in odd places. First it had swallowed me down crevices on the sidewalks of Boston and then, popping me back out of some contiguous underground catacomb, I appeared unclothed, on this Canadian Highway. I imagined what I looked like from the opposite lane: the new freedom of my life was more than I had bargained for. In Michigan, I put my silk blouse and straight black skirt back on again, had a cigarette to practice talking to myself this time, and got myself the postdoctoral job.

This day following the divorce, Candy and I went to the gas station to pick up the U-Haul for me to go to Michigan. She drove it with me following, to the house where we met some U-Haul movers who helped me move my piano into the truck. Bryan stood and watched. I tried not to dissolve in infuriation. We then drove to the apartment, where we loaded everything else that I was taking. Bryan followed us over. He said he had come for one of the couches. Going to the kitchen, he reached for the box of spices and sat himself on the living room floor, the box in front of him and began separating them into two piles, one for him and one for me he said, simultaneously watching while we loaded the truck. Incredulous, I closed the back of the U-Haul and thanked him for not helping as I waved goodbye and left him with both stacks of spice bottles.

Pulling out of the apartment driveway, we started for Michigan: Candy, driving the U-Haul; Monica driving her car; and I, mine. Both girls, Kelly and Alisha, were riding in the U-Haul. Within minutes of leaving, Candy disappeared into the traffic. I couldn't tell whether she was ahead of me or behind me. I hurried and slowed alternately, looking forwards or backwards all the time, trying to find her. Driving, I stopped at nearly every pay telephone booth in a collection of cable-connected dots directed north on the interstate to call Bryan. In a string of phone-booth goodbyes, as I was fast disappearing from view, I would ask only if Candy had called him yet to find me.

By the time I arrived in Lansing, Michigan, some five hours later, Candy was already unloading the U-Haul. She had found the university housing where I was to be staying. We all spent the night spread around the apartment, having unpacked it all, and Candy and Monica left the next day while I started work.

I learned quickly to hate my small apartment. I told myself that it didn't matter, none of it, kids' three-wheelers, cockroaches, laundromats, screaming babies, working so hard. I had been here before. We all had; living like a graduate student was not a new experience. In a few months, new friends named it The Hovel. Living there, I was becoming more certain each day that it mattered irrevocably. The weight of my thought increased with its daily repetition. The point was just that: I had been here before and here I was again. I had started to care how and where I lived too late: this was the point beyond return and the thought made a tight constant knot in my hair, on top just next to my scalp.

At night, going home late after working, sometimes after midnight I would drive around town, away from campus in the residential areas. At first I would do it just to avoid going back to my apartment. Then I noticed I was looking into the lit windows of the residents' houses where I drove. I bought hanging plants to line the front large window of my apartment. Behind the row of plants, I was in hiding in the greenery. I knew, even so, it could get worse than this: in the summer, shopping in Cincinnati at a factory-outlet store that Monica and I had heard was in the heart of downtown and part of a real skid row, I had grabbed Kelly and Monica each by the hand, shortly after we were inside, telling that that we must leave. "We have to get out of here, now," I had said without explanation.

Kelly, without budging, at a low rack of Cincinnati Reds baseball shirts, said to me. "But, Mom, we just got here. I've been wanting a baseball shirt all summer."

Monica, taking on her sisterly aspect and playing aunt to Kelly, drew her aside. "You know your mother is having a hard time these days, so let's go and don't give her a hard time now." In fact, Monica had suggested not coming at all, wondering if I was up to an out-of-town trip, as she put it. I tried to explain to her about slipping, here right on skid row, into it. It would be merciless. That could happen, I explained, if I wasn't able to work again. If I wasn't able to concentrate enough to do it. Monica was looking at the sweat breaking out on my face and arms. She grabbed me, in the armpits, both of us wondering if I would really pass out, and called to Kelly, "Come on, Kell, get yourself a baseball shirt in a hurry. Your mom says it's OK." She was speaking across the racks and reaching into her purse for some money simultaneously.

She sat me on curb while she went for the car. Kelly was subdued, and we all rode silently to the first McDonald's past the skid row exit.

Now on my nightly rides, I came across a redwood house, topped with skylights, on the very edge of town. It, with its grand piano, became my favorite. Once a night I pretended this house was mine. I thought of it as penance for every comment of scathing I had previously made about living in a regular residential neighborhood on or off of Air Force bases. Coming from the closest corner I would slow before passing, to prepare for a good look, then I would speed up to a normal pace and cruise past, sloshing in homelessness more tangible to me than rain on the streets in those nights, wondering how it had all come about that I was without everything familiar, including most of all, my own daughter. Bryan and I had brought it about. We were equal parties to it. There was the fact, and I was learning to wait for the terrible year without her, to end.

Like it or not, this was, in fact, the scientific chance of my lifetime; it would perhaps be almost anyone's in this decade of the 1980's, the birth of recombinant DNA technology. Anyone at all in biological science, not having learned it by the California grapevine where it was developed, would have to find another means. I was coming out of my own scientific oblivion into a field that would intimidate uninitiated biological scientists all over the country and who would go begging to learn it. I, who was wondering about concentrating beyond dishwashing, would learn from those who took if off the ground in the first place on the West Coast.

Michigan State University had managed to entice two young molecular biologists straight from the California Institute of Technology, who together would teach the most sought-after summer course in the country at Cold Spring Harbor Labs on Long Island. Recombinant DNA Technology. I would be lucky enough to learn it in their labs.

In Michigan, working without Kelly with me, I spent the first few months in twelve hour days regularly, learning the ins and outs of recombinant DNA technology on the spot. Just beginning now, in more ways than one, I was much slower than everyone else in the lab. They had had a year's introduction. I often had to repeat parts of experiments due to my mistakes, and I would go back to the lab at night to work, more slowly and methodically, alone. Painstakingly and to my amazement, I began to learn it. I was learning to clone genes. Mid-year I completed some work begun earlier by a technician which at the time, was somewhat of a technological milestone. The idea had been formulated at Cold Spring Harbor the summer before. The word spread quickly in the Biochemistry Department, students and faculty came to congratulate me, and I was famous on the fifth floor of the university's biochemistry building for a day.

20

OH CANADA

Shortly before we were divorced, Bryan told me that the day would come that I would thank him for making us both go through with it. In truth, it happened one day, a few years hence from our divorce — I had to wait awhile — but it happened: it occurred one day when I was driving across the Ambassador Bridge between Detroit, Michigan, and Windsor, Canada. I spoke out loud and thanked Bryan to my windshield, passing the pair of American and Canadian flags fixed, high over the Detroit River, to the midpoint of the steel lattice.

Doing it, I remembered the night I made Bryan and Bill Anderson go to see Bill Evans one night in San Francisco. They both teased me mercilessly. Bill's girlfriend went along with the fun. It had to do with how I'd had to see him, the most famous jazz pianist of all times, living or dead, but at a place the gas station attendant said was too dangerous for us to go. Going, there, in that rough part of town was the part of the evening Bryan enjoyed. The rest of us were reluctant about it: it was in a bad part of town, on the end of Divisadero Street, and the door was locked. Bill Evans himself was late getting there. Until he arrived, crowding into the storefront entry way for protection and peering in the barred windows of the door, we weren't even sure we had the right place. But Bryan persuaded us all to wait. Sure enough, Bill Evans himself showed up. And Bryan got us in there to see him in person. It was a lifetime dream, for me, come true. And it was a night, I decided — for me anyway — that we went too far in our giving each other a hard time. By then, the joke had gotten lost.

The Ambassador Bridge between the U.S. and Canada in Detroit is like a miniature Golden Gate and is hung with lights, bulbous as Japanese Lanterns of a garden party: they follow the dips of the spans and they lean away from the wind on their cables; they will usually be on in the early evening before the sun is completely set, always lit when I come in the winter then, and there in Canada, a country that is not my own and city of dusky streets, a place

I can lose myself, I will take one piano lesson, and then another. And then as regularly as a catechism on Sundays, whatever day of the week this, I will come every other week and climb the stairs to the studio, for a jazz piano lesson. From a man who can play anything.

For once I will be able watch close-up where the hands go on white-and-black keys, even while I can't see all the notes fast enough or hear them well enough, or begin to put them together in my head. I can ask him to play it again, and I will be inalterably glad to be alive again.

He has a three foot poster of Beethoven in his younger years over his piano. On it below, he plays mostly jazz: his own obsession. The light is dim over his piano summer or winter, but he can play it in the complete dark. There isn't any jazz great he can't mimic, even Bill Evans himself, but that's not the point; mostly he has a style of his own that now I would know anywhere without watching his hands or seeing him at all. Other students, musicians, and band roadmen say that since they can remember, he has always sounded like he plays with four hands, although I like to listen to him best when he plays — barely accompanying himself — a single-note melody.   He has a drawerful of television and film soundtracks he wrote during some time that he worked for the Canadian Broadcasting Company and he writes jingles for ads with the same care that he writes soundtracks and plays straight-ahead jazz.

My friends and I go sometimes and hear him play in bands all around town. Now we know most of the clubs in Detroit and Windsor — a myriad mirrors of his reflection dark at a piano, although the intensity in his face sometimes comes at odd times, not always when he is playing — sometimes I go alone to the bars just as I have gone to some outdoor concerts and performances in those summers. If I am lucky, I will walk up the steps to his studio on a windy winter evening, one day early for my lesson, and hear him through the slit of light in the door frame, playing, his own favorite, Yesterdays: for himself, a Jerome Kern standard, an old tune rarely recognized, and for an audience just perhaps, upon request: John Lennon and Paul McCartney come back — Yesterdays just one more time — perhaps one time more plaintively than before. Bryan might be heard to say that an artsy craftsy guy like him figures, and I would have to say, yes; yes, it does, doesn't it?

21

COLLEEN AGAIN

MARCH 5, 1988

A make-up table is something I have only recently acquired — on the surface of it — a place to sit and primp. In having one now I am copying my friend Connie. Hers is in a spot beside her vanity basin (sink is how I really think of it) with a nice big round flip-flop mirror, one that shows you at your regular size and one that doubles your size, for close work, and a great wing-backed chair that for years has had pieces of stuffing popping out here and there on both its arms and its seat. Connie has long planned to recover it, as it originally belonged to her mother-in-law, whom she loved dearly, and whose presence, according to the family, is still close-in, in that chair.

Connie usually sits, half-dressed, getting ready for work whether it be teaching school, or working at the main Dayton department store, stockinged and shoed, dressing from the feet up, as many of us seem to do, legs crossed, doing her make-up. That's how the kids said it.

Before I knew Connie, I had never seen so many bottles, lipsticks, mascaras, eye shadows, puffs, little drawers of her vanity filled with discarded or sought-after items of make-up. Leaning forward in that great winged chair, pursing her lips, and peering at her eye shadow sideways, she would talk to all of us, simultaneously often rolling or unrolling her hair in hot rollers, me and all of our kids, lying criss-cross on the bed like sloths slung sideways, with me struggling for my own edge in a pile of teenagers and pre-teenagers, limbs dangling at all angles and bodies in partial headstands at times: all of us, seemingly a new age of Moms and children, all discussing topics more embarrassing to the mothers than to the children who, media-inured, don't mind all talking at once.

5:15 PM: *It has been twenty-one years now today since Colleen was killed: there's no hiding from the fact; she has been dead as many years as she was alive. The symmetry is quite awful - I rush to write as though to rid myself of these hours, starting with 5:15, to put them on a conveyor belt out of town: ice-crackling terror, being run out of town, this time of this day, every year.   My daughter, college student now, as petit as I am tall, born two years to the quarter hour, not of the official time of the crash, but of the start of Colleen's end of innocence and of my yearly terror — the boarding of the airplane — is on a date this evening.   She is an auburn-haired beauty, my friends tell me. This is her 19th birthday.*

So, now I have my own make-up table. It is a converted end table with a round rotating flip-flop mirror, that turns me from life-size to twice life-size and back again, for close work, and it is where Kelly, at nineteen, is likely to ask me important questions, the ones she is otherwise reluctant to pose. When I am sitting at it cross-legged in long socks or stockings, feeling more like an adult woman then than I do most other times in my life, she slides by my door quickly and shoots her questions, passing briefly in and out of sight.

"Hey mother," mother and hey, both telltale signs of a question slow to be raised, "I was wondering..."

"So what is it?"

"Well, since I'm going to college this fall and there will be no hours in the dorm," (I already obviously know the question), "I was thinking that it would make more sense if I got used to having no hours while I was still at home, rather than just moving into a dorm and suddenly having no hours at all, overnight, so to speak. If you know what I mean?"

"You mean," I say, "Try it out before school?" I form it into a succinct sentence now that the subject has bobbed up (thanks to her) and down (thanks to me) a few times before, since her high school graduation.

8:15 PM: The clock says it — 8:15. Twenty-one years ago this moment, in the Green Door I lay on the bottom bunk while Bryan puttered in the living room. From the wedding reception it was the first quiet moment of the day. I remember I had folded my hands on my chest and said to myself that she is there by now. Not quite 8:30. She was there all right. My old pain still gets me in cynicism sometimes. I hurry now, to get through the next hours - 8:15 until 11:30 - when it had already happened but before the airlines had notified my parents and Colleen had lain in the snowy field as I had lain in my bunk.

Now, for her 19th birthday I have bought Kelly a dressing table — from a place like K-Mart, a spindly wrought-iron table with an attached mirror for doubling your size, the whole thing being perhaps one yard wide and eighteen inches deep. Ridiculously wiry in its stance, with no seeming center of gravity, all glass on top and a second shelf of glass below the top one, it is bound to fall into a thousand pieces: a wrought-iron and glass heap on its first trip from dorm to apartment, apartment to dorm, wherever her doubtless vagabond existence in the next years, will take her. That had been the basis for my buying it at a place like K-Mart. Perhaps I shall return it and not give it to her for her birthday. Perhaps I'll let it sit in my basement while she grows up altogether. I, the biologist, I want so badly to interject it as a heritable trait, what it carries with its glass and wrought iron, into her life, so that she can learn from me early on what I only learned so recently, about learning to live, one day at a time, from my friend Connie.

22

THE ASTRONAUT AGAIN

JANUARY 18, 1987

The moments of the Challenger accident, I was standing in an ice cream shoppe just off campus, at Michigan State University where I work. There was a TV running on the counter below the cash register. I could hear the usual count-down. Actually it was a repeat of the countdown, as the Challenger had already blown up in mid-air. Not knowing, I asked Frank, the shoppe owner, if it had gotten off yet, and I leaned over to take a look at the TV screen, where all I saw was a shot of the empty ocean.

"There has just been a bad, bad, accident," he said. I asked what had happened, and he repeated all that he knew; what had happened and what was happening now was unclear. Like everyone else, I said I couldn't believe it. I went back to my lab, where work had stopped in all the labs, with everyone listening to the radio reports.

That night I ran through the gate arm of the parking lot, and I nearly ran over two people: a woman coming out of an alley and a child on a street corner. I went the next day to lunch with a group of friends and in response to one friend's commenting on the difficulties of women in science as a profession, I began a diatribe on what I considered to be opportunities for women in science that had existed forever.

I cited Madame Curie. There were, after all, no laws, contrary to what women thought, about keeping women out of science. I thought of the movie, The Strawberry Statement, in which Elliot Gould played a graduate student going for a Ph.D. in English and blowing it at his final exam by finally telling his committee what he thought of their calling F. Scott Fitzgerald names. Then he had gotten up on the examination table and walked on it, continuing vociferously, with the committee still in place around it. I thought of Bryan's telling me about the instructor pilot who walked on the table on top of his checklist, and I thought of how I wanted to do like both Elliot Gould and Bryan on the night of President Nixon's dinner when we were at the table with General and Mrs. Scowcroft. Right now my voice was very loud and easily I could see myself walking on this table at lunch.

This time I went to a psychiatrist on my own to ask what was my problem. He answered in one word: grief. I shook my head and looked sideways, and said I'd think about it.

Dear Bryan:

I have, in fact, thought about it and decided that the day of the Challenger, of all days, was probably the day I believed most that you had died, for me, the reason being, that I think there was a real fork in the road back there for us in 1979 when you went for your NASA interview. The Challenger fork was the one I wanted us to take then. I thought it would be a way for us to save ourselves. You would finally have gotten your heart's desire to be an astronaut, and I could have gotten mine, a chance to learn recombinant DNA technology. I could have found a position at Baylor University and learned it all there, instead of here. I was thinking so hard about it then that I even remember the biohazard containment sign I saw on a door of one of the labs where I was looking while you were at your interview.

We could have bought one of those beautiful condominiums where all the astronauts and their families lived, outside of NASA, around that little lake: the grass there seemed appropriately unreal: taller than usual, and greener and lusher than the stuff they put in Easter Egg baskets. And the lake was aqua-colored. At the motel I saw a female candidate I later knew was Sally Ride, jogging. Three of the astronauts on the Challenger were names I recognized on the list of candidates you brought home from the interview. I thought that it would be our last chance, and I was sure it was the chance to save ourselves.

I was the only one left by then, except your old friend, Bob, who thought you should do it. Even you were dubious by this time, and you didn't have much regard for the science projects assigned to the astronauts waiting to fly. Afterwards, you told me I should have applied too. Bob Crippen asked you to sit next to him at dinner, and you didn't know who he was until after it was all over — you weren't really taking it seriously, so why did you bother to go at all I later wondered. You left there telling the board you weren't interested in a mission specialist position, only a pilot position. You had left here saying you would never fly anything unless it were a single-seater again, not even the space shuttle. A mission specialist position would be fine. You lasted 45 minutes in that whirling Barone chair, longer without vomiting than anyone the guy running it that day had seen anyone last. 7000 people had applied; they interviewed 200, took 20, and I can see now that, if you had gone for it — leaving out the Krista McCullough teacher — you might well have been one of the three real astronauts from that 1979 group who were on the Challenger when it blew up.

Sincerely,
Layne

23

THE WAR AGAIN

JULY 18, 1986

Alexandria - a thousand dust-tormented streets. Flies and beggars own it today, and those who enjoy an intermediate existence in between. Someone once said that Alexandria was the great wine press of love; those who emerged from it were the sick men, the solitaries, the prophets -

Justine,
by Lawrence Durell

In the summer of l986, thirteen years later, it all started again with a telephone call from a friend.   I was in the lab at the time. This was a friend whose brother had gone to Vietnam, so he knew more about the war than most.

"Have you seen the MIA article in the Free Press," he asked me. He had lived in Detroit for years and still read the Detroit Free Press. Since living here, I had noticed all of Michigan read the Free Press regularly.

"Of course not," I answered, abruptly, simultaneously wanting and not wanting to know what he was talking about.

"It's about the MIAs of Michigan," Mike went on, "There are seventy-five of them, and it is about them and their families. It has pictures of all of them too."

"So who were they all," I ask. I couldn't think of what to say. I knew who they were. Somehow the whole country was confused. The POWs and MIAs were not the Army guys of Platoon and Rambo was its own farce. It was back in my head again. Nor were they the Vietnam Vets as everyone knew them. In fact, reporters and other busy-bodies didn't know what or who they were talking about. The real POWs were invisible. Individually and collectively, except for a few who had run for office. Former pilots and air crew members, that was who they were, and they were not speaking about the war: not yet anyway.   I left the lab and walked back to my office, an up-garret like room, back from the labs themselves. Not unsurprisingly, I felt it start in my legs. My walking was accompanied by a sensation of head-long bodily plummetting.

That evening I read a Detroit Free Press for myself, and I got into my car to head downtown, Lansing Michigan, for a candlelight service for the MIAs of Michigan, on the steps of the Capitol Building. The Michigan Vietnam Vets were there, and they took me in with no questions asked. The speaker added the name of John Dearborn, from California, to the list that he intoned into the darkness by name and Michigan hometown. They gave me a lit candle along with the Michigan MIA families, and after the ceremony was over I blew it out, put it into the pocket of my jacket, and the next morning I boarded an airplane for Washington; the reservation I had already booked and broken twice: I was going in order to attend the POW/MIA gathering of families in Alexandria, Virginia. Held by the National League of Families, an organization started in the late 1960s by the families themselves, members had been meet-ing annually in Washington both before and after the end of the war to discuss POW/MIA issues.

This year's national meeting had engendered the Free Press article of a day earlier about Michigan members and their MIAs. It was to be held at the Mark Radisson Hotel in Alexandria, Virginia. The article had photos and interviews with families of the seventy-five MIAs from Michigan.

In two hours' time I stepped from a taxi onto the side-walk at the Mark Radisson Hotel, some five or ten miles from downtown Washington, set back in an island of trees but so close to the interstate heading down toward Virginia, you could still hear the traffic. From the curb I could see an atrium, high and as arched as the ceiling of a cathedral, hung with plants and chandeliers. The window on the side where I got out of the cab, was wall-sized. Through it I could see the woods again on the other side. The door was strangely angled at the top. Entering, I wend-ed my way through the crowd in the lobby back toward what I found to be the main ballroom, where the meetings were being held, counting the chandeliers as I went and thinking as I passed a single counter bar on the right side of the lobby that a gin and tonic would taste good at this point, even at l0 AM.

The lobby spread in every direction: couches, lounge chairs, end tables, table lamps, and standing lamps, set on ornamental rugs over a slate slab floor, a means of averting one's eyes from the nametags of the MIA families. I looked in the direction of the ballroom and headed toward a crowd between two sets of double doors. It was just l0:30 as I stepped inside the double doors: it may as well have been a scientific meeting of the kind to which I was accustomed, with the speaker droning, bending over a small podium light, rows and rows of people shuffling in wooden chairs, looking minute in the huge room. Coughing and throat clearing among audience members were noticeable, inter-rupting the speaker's slide presentation. The speaker fin-ished, lights came on, and two aisles became visible; each had a microphone placed midway toward the speaker's podium. The ballroom was enormous.

A Defense Intelligence Agency speaker, whom I later knew as Mr. Salvatore Ferro, Chief of its External Affairs branch, had been presenting overheads at the end of the talk when I came in, consisting of statistics of what I was to learn were termed "live sightings" of possible American POWs in Vietnam. He had concluded just as I found an empty seat in the dark. Rather than joining the rest of the speakers on the platform, he apparently was leaving alto-gether, as he gathered his material and left the room. I moved after him, following him into the lobby and up the escalator to a mezzanine above it. The main floor, half of a story below, seemed close compared with the six stories open to the skylight at the top of the hotel. I introduced myself as briefly as possible and told him that I had missed the major portion of his presentation. "Do you suppose that you could repeat the information just on that last overhead?" I felt somewhat apologetic.

"Not at all."

I was surprised at his kindliness as he laid his briefcase flat on the balcony railing and stated that the statistics were best summarized on the overhead itself. I looked over the railing at the emptied lobby; the numbers were 400 reported citings since l972, of which 64 were credited to potential POWs. "Of those," he said, "59 have proven most likely to be fallacious, so l4 accounts have been maintained as potential Americans held."

"Does each reported citing require corroboration by a second individual in order for you to consider it substantial enough to list?"

He said that it did not, but that often a citing occurred when individuals were together in a group so that usually it happened that more than one individual had witnessed any given situation.

"Could I ask you a question you've been asked a thousand times? About a specific individual? However, this person would be more easily identifiable, I think, as he is black."

"Certainly , what is his name?"

I said the name the first time aloud to someone it would have concrete meaning to, in many years. "His name is Major John Dearborn. He was the electronics warfare officer on the last B-52 shot down over Hanoi, in l972. The Christmas bombings."

"December the 26th, am I right?"

"Yes," I said, startled to be talking with someone who knew about it. "His crew thought that he himself, or his body, was in the possession of the North Vietnamese."

"Yes, I must say, I am familiar with his name." said Mr. Ferro, "You may find that hard to believe, since there are more than 2500 listed MIAs. However, I don't recall more detailed information about Major Dearborn at the moment."

"There was never any more information about him after they were in the Hanoi Hilton, the night they took them in. But that night, the North Vietnamese knew who he was even as they interrogated the crew about him."

"Yes, it was rather unusual."

He went on. "To my knowledge, there has been a live citing report on one black man, shot down in l972. However this person was shot down over Laos, in a high performance aircraft, making it unlikely that it was, in fact, Major Dearborn." He was taking a business card out of his wallet. "If you would care to call me at my office I would be glad to look into it and to answer any specific questions about Major Dearborn that I can. I'll look into his file."

The business card, which I mistakenly thought for months was fuchsia in color — until I looked in my desk drawer for it and found it to be white like the rest — I poked into the jacket of my pocket. I was pushing both pockets at the seams, the card pressed against my thighs through the thicknesses of my jacket and skirt, arms straightened. I looked over the railing again. Perhaps Mr. Ferro didn't know a thing more, and for sure, Ellen Dearborn would know as much or more than he knew, I didn't even know where Ellen was now, or her children who must be grown, but, and I couldn't speak of John himself, only of John's name; in his name and for his sake; try it again, in his name and for my own sake, it was, I knew now, that I had come.

I thanked Mr. Ferro and rode the escalator back to the main floor where tables outside the ballroom were set up for display, strewn with posters, literature, paraphernalia, POW/MIA T-shirts, key chains, flags, mugs, bumper stickers. Just like any convention with vendors selling their wares, chattering, chattering, bending, turning, chattering, and then selling. Only the lobby was empty now. My heart was pounding again, and I blinked slowly seeing a bumper sticker as familiar as those on the table in front of me, plain white on black, stating POW/MIA, were unfamiliar; a sticker that must have been 14 years old at least, POWS NEVER HAVE A NICE DAY; I had seen it on a Lincoln Continental, not anywhere near 14 years old, on the Long Island Freeway just a month before.

I had been driving my friend Eleanor's BMW, her precious BMW, to the Cold Spring Harbor Laboratories, on Long Island, for meetings, the thing being that the man in the Lincoln Continental — he was also good-looking — had passed me at a speed greater than I could even guess, perhaps more than 90 miles an hour. He had glanced in my direction and looked back again, once past me. I felt the slight push of my own foot on my (Eleanor's) accelerator and looked again. A bumper sticker on the right rear bumper of his Lincoln said it incredibly — POWS NEVER HAVE A NICE DAY — and I saw again, from my own past, my own junky Datsun station wagon for which, even meaning to do it, I had never gotten the sticker in the days when the issue was acceptable, 1972. I floored the gas pedal: who was he, a father, a brother, a son, a husband, or just some jerk driving someone else's car. The sticker was older in make than the car - that was the hitch.

The sticker had been plastered all over the Northern California freeways, bumper to bumper, in the winter of l972 and the spring of l973. When President Nixon had ordered the bombing of Hanoi, that December and the close of the war came, the question had then been, would the North Vietnamese release the American POWs? And Californians, all, whatever they thought of the war, pasted up the bumper sticker. But even Eleanor's BMW could not keep pace with this man in his Continental.

What was my plan, anyway? None of course. To force him off the road? He would imagine that I was trying to tell him that he had a flat tire or a dragging muffler, or some such if I motioned to the rear of his car. Or he could imagine that I was trying to pick him up. Then, getting out of the car, were he actually to stop, what would I say?

I saw your bumper sticker and wondered if you might be from California?

I saw your bumper sticker and wondered if you might be free tonight?

I saw your bumper sticker and, whoever you are, I heard there was someone come for those of us who - if you'll pardon my use of the phrase - are heavy-laden from the war, and I just wondered if you might give me a ride a ways?

The Continental was going at a speed somewhat greater than 100 miles per hour, it was a fact, because I was doing 90 in Eleanor's car. Watching it, I may as well have been standing still, as it drew away with ease.

24

THE PAKSE C-130

Mr. Ferro's presentation on the program was listed as **POW Live Sightings**. Next on the program, following the Defense Intelligence Agency presentation of Mr. Ferro, was something termed **CIL Presentation**. Speaking first was a Major Webb, Commanding Officer of CIL, which I was to learn was an acronym for the Central Identification Laboratory. It was located in the Philippine Islands at Clark Air Force Base. I wondered randomly how long CIL had been in existence.

The presentation by Major Webb consisted of a series of slides showing the actual excavation of what was called the Pakse crash site in Laos. This was a C-130 crash site. Called a gunship, the C-130 carried the largest crew of any of the Air Force planes in the war. The number of the crew, unlike other Air Force planes most of which carried one or two crew members, was not fixed in the C-130. Carrying a crew of ten or more, it was the only plane that had a crew larger than the B-52. One such C-130 gunship was equipped for the president: a presidential safety place, albeit in the sky, in case of war in the U.S. and possible bombing of Washington. Didn't I, in fact, know too that they were used over Vietnam for special reconnaissance, not unlike the SR-71. However, in the C-130s the high technology equipment consisted not of SR-71-type cameras capable of producing photographs of small objects clearly at 80,000 ft., but of infrared equipment which, heat-seeking, could detect a living organism or organisms on the ground. With the exception of the presidential model, the C-130s flew reconnaissance over North Vietnam and over Laos. The Pakse crash site, being discussed at the moment in this CIL Presentation, was in Laos. Thirteen crew members had been carried as missing in action for fifteen years.

Like so many matters of scientific achievement that do not involve study at a molecular level, whether physical or biological, I was taken aback to see the difficulties in accomplishing the task of unearthing the Pakse C-130.

The slides I watched carefully. They showed a small

bulldozer scraping the ground of an ordinary field.   It did not look at all as I had imagined it.I had expected snarls of undergrowth, overgrowth, mysterious types of vegetation; I imagined gnarled, no-name trees, thwarted in right angles of their attempted growth towards the sky; they would easily fit into the prevalent sort of paintings one sees in churches of Jesus among the olive trees in his Holy Land.

I had reason to think of Laos as a strange land. Bryan had talked of it with some respect, of the danger of being shot down over it due to the impossibility of rescue. Later I thought, considering my strong image of the terrain, he apparently feared the possibility more than others. From his talk, I had come to imagine Laos as a literal black hole for U.S. pilots because they disappeared into it and never seemed to return;   nor were they heard about or from, rarely even on the POW tap-code roster. This was according to other pilots.

I had never heard, myself, of friendly helicopters picking up downed pilots in Laos or even of F-4 phantoms — the F-4s screaming and ominous in appearance to everyone because of their bird-like drooping wings and because of their after-burners that looked like the open holes of blast furnaces: ominous in appearance, that is, to everyone except the downed, doomed, if you will, pilots, the compatriots who went after them, and the ground crews that sent them, as was said by the F-4 flyers, screaming — I had never hear of F-4 phantoms flying reconnaissance over Laos.

As I had understood it, being shot down over, or even near, Laos was a phenomenon to be even less desired than being shot down over downtown Hanoi. There, you knew you would probably stay in the Hilton, but there were no known camps, only alleged ones, in Laos.

In the photographs Major Webb was showing the land was flat, weedy, and seemingly, exceedingly hard. Digging looked arduous, even without the aid of a soundtrack to accompany the photos. This digging was followed by a sifting using what is best described as oversized kitchen strainers. The sifted, particulate matter, then presumably was packaged for return to the CIL for inspection and identification.

The chief forensic anthropologist at the CIL was a Dr. Furue whose presentation also consisted of a series of slides; lists of the scrutinizable characteristics for which these small pieces of bone were arranged, under lights, on what resembled anatomy class-like dissecting tables. His was a how-to presentation: the identification of bone bits among the rubble. He mentioned no crew member names.

At the conclusion of both Major Webb's and Dr. Furue's presentations the floor was opened to questions. A lovely blond young woman, posed a question to Dr. Furue concerning these fragments that had been sifted out from the dirt and debris. She asked how large they were off the screen and how he could determine that they, any of them, belonged to any particular individual. Dr. Furue was from Thailand, I later learned, and not only was he very soft-spoken, but his English was very difficult to understand.

It seemed strange to hear him use the word dime in his answer, this small oriental man, all the more, perhaps, because it was the only word in the sentences of his answer that I comprehended. Apparently it was a word in English which he was somewhat comfortable using, yet one had difficulty imagining him, handling literal silver dimes of change. In none of the subsequent questions and answers was I able to understand the English of any of Dr. Furue's explanations. My mind wandered. Straining still to understand Dr. Furue, I went back to the larger items, the first CIL slide presentation, by Major Webb.

In none of his slides had there been evidence of airplane parts. Presumably they had been cleared years ago by the Laotians, and presumably whatever had not been cleared had simply disintegrated and melded with the land.

The actual matter of the original airplane whereabouts itself was unclear, and it was a valid question as not all of the crew, perhaps none of the crew, now that I thought of it, would necessarily have gotten out of the airplane. And if they had gotten out, however one did that in a C-130, they wouldn't necessarily have been in the field all at one site.

My heart was pounding once more. I felt a slow dreadful apprehension moving in even though I knew the facts were all steady in the past tense. I was seeing, right before me, the whole thing, the ugly and the beautiful, the beautiful and the damned: siftings, solid spindrift, little bone bits out of the Laotian fields on a white-clothed table and the table on a screen; a Smithsonian-like anthropological display. Each piece was tagged, and decreasing or increasing in size depending upon which way you looked across the screen; all were opposite the lovely blond girl at the microphone: who was she, the daughter, the sister, not the wife or mother of a pilot because she was too young and not the lover, because this microphone was designated for family members only.

I got up and left the ballroom. I knew that if the whole country could be attending this convention, all 200 million odd of us jam-packed into this ballroom — not just members of National League of Families — then, half of us, easily, would say what is the use of even discussing it; include for consideration the live sightings perhaps and exclude the excavations among the bones, whether incomplete or complete, unidentifiable or identifiable, in skeletons for each bearer, what is the point? we would say.

The CIL Presentation was apparently over because the lobby was filling. I stepped back from a drinking fountain, deliberately listening to a nearby conversation. It was bordering on a dispute. It concerned the dime-sized bone fragments. I overheard a tall red-haired man exclaiming: "You can't use what they call bone fragments to identify anyone!" His voice was very intense.

"Do you know how they do it?" I turned, without introducing myself, and asked.

"It's impossible," he stated, "At least in my opinion."

He went on. "Unless the bone fragments are large enough to be identifiable as belonging together so they can be separated from those belonging to another individual, or unless they can be chemically tested in order to distinguish the bones of one individual compositionally from those of another. Otherwise I think it would be impossible to make an identification with any certainty." My own thought for the past minutes had been that surface qualities of texture and color just wouldn't get it. Carbon-dating, all I knew about dating items from the past, wouldn't serve a useful purpose here either.

The man I was talking with was a dentist, the brother of a crew member. We talked chemistry and agreed; you really needed fresh bone to do much chemistry. Otherwise it was a bug-a-boo. Meanwhile, distractedly, I was thinking of the girl and the Thai doctor.

"You know," this dentist said, "There were fourteen men on that C-130."

I stumbled on my own voice, "Then why are there just thirteen sets of remains?"

"Because the l4th was taken alive they think." I felt my breath catch and didn't try to speak. He went on, "They think he got hung up in a tree and lost an arm. My question is why didn't they find bone fragments from his arm? Why aren't there fourteen sets of remains?"

"I'll tell you why," he answered his own question, "Because the anthropologist was told these were remains from a crew of thirteen."

25

MRS. PARKER

Later that afternoon, on the very center couch — its back toward the bar where I had stopped for the gin and tonic — I sat listening to a Mrs. Parker describe why she had refused to attend a meeting concerning the Pakse crash excavation. With the exception of Mrs. Parker, myself, and a reporter, who apparently was a personal friend of the family, the lobby was deserted. She and I were sitting on either ends of the couch, while the reporter was pacing in regular rhythm in front of a group of large planters to its side. The agitation of both seemed mutual, although Mrs. Parker was doing most of the talking. The shaft of white from the hotel skylight some floors above formed a cone around the three of us: we were looking out through a downward spray of dust particles delineated by the sun. The anguish of Mrs. Parker was in her voice, I thought, not looking at her and in the appearance of the reporter, reflected from her face to his as he paced the floor.

Mrs. Parker had recently refused to accept the remains of her husband Colonel Parker, delivered by the Air Force from the CIL with what was termed a positive identification of his remains. Before the arrival of the reporter, she talked to me of calling in academic forensic anthropologists whose report confirmed her own appraisal of the remains, and both were in contradiction to the CIL report. In the anthropologists' formal evaluation, it was stated that a positive identification of Colonel Parker could not be made. Colonel Parker had been aboard the C-130 that had crashed in Pakse, and the meeting of family members concerned all the crew members of that C-130.

I realized, as we were talking, that I had seen Mrs. Parker on television a few days earlier, with a nephew speaking on her behalf and on behalf of the family, regarding the discrepancies between the forensic reports by CIL and by the academic sector. While we talked, the lobby virtually deserted from the afternoon's meetings, another informal meeting was taking place in a conference room on some higher floor, restricted to families of the Pakse crash site. The National League Board members had not agreed to Mrs. Parker's carrying a tape recorder to this meeting, hence her decision not to attend.

According to Mrs. Parker, Colonel Brooks, Chairman of the Board of the National League had himself taken the remains of his own son to their family dentist for confirmation of the report from CIL. She did not understand why, then, he would have an objection to her recording the proceedings of this meeting. The reporter echoed her concern. Many family members were expressing similar concerns, now that other aircraft crash sites were starting to be excavated. Clearly the problem would be similar with B-52 crash sites, which reportedly were on the list provided by the North Vietnamese, in an agreement concerning future sites of potential excavations. Clearly as well, the problem would exist for any crash site, even that of a single-seat jet: a positive identification would require more than evidence of human bone material in the vicinity of a reported jet, bomber, or other aircraft crash. It had been reported that some thought bones reported as belonging to American pilots actually belonged to Asian land residents. The implication of the journalist was that Mrs. Parker, although alone in speaking out, was not alone among MIA families in her questioning of the performance of the CIL in this regard.

As the two of them left, I was alone in the lobby. Leafing through the pages of the program, the agenda for Saturday and Sunday, I knew without turning the pages back to Thursday and Friday that I wished I had come for the entire meeting.

When I had called the National League of Families number in Washington, a recording had given me the telephone number of the Mark Radisson Hotel in Alexandria, Virginia, where everyone even then was gathering on Wednesday.

Calling the hotel itself, the clerk on duty at the time told me there were no open reservations available but that families were free to double up as best they could and that yes, there were many families of returned POWs attending, along with the MIA families.

I asked him to check a few names, but none I inquired about was due to register. The force of the past narrowed itself into the telephone line in the voice of the Mark

Radisson Hotel clerk — I had peered closely at the one on duty when I had arrived — suspicious of anyone who, in seconds, could bring me to such a collapse of time, a voice ringing through the telephone line into the canyon, a language - POW/MIA - I hadn't spoken in thirteen years and which no one I knew now even knew I spoke. Double up, yes, hide in a high hotel room, over that chandeliered cathedralled ceiling, kneel and pray at bedside in a pool of dark in the night lights of Washington, for the guts to stay, the guts to go, or to have come at all, the guts sliding in retrospect already threatening to be my undoing; kneel and pray, then climb into bed amidst a roomful of familiar faces who spoke the language of a collapsed past, a present collapsing into the past.

26

JANE FONDA

Ever since my arrival in Alexandria at the Mark Radisson Hotel, I had not seen anyone familiar. I had learned that there was a Michigan Delegation flown here from Suffrage Air Force Base outside of Detroit, and I spoke to the Air Force major in charge of the group to ask if there might be a way for me to ride back on their military transport going back into Detroit the next day. Without orders, he said, it was not possible. I had known the answer in the moment of my asking. Even in the Air Force itself, contrary to what most people thought, one had to be a pilot or crew member to hop rides with no orders. But it did not matter so much today. I had a reservation for the evening; my only real regret was having missed the meeting of the day prior, the afternoon session at 4:30 entitled **Greetings from the Veterans.**

Four returned POWs had given speeches in the afternoon, but it was the last by Captain Richard Stratton I regretted missing the most. Before Bryan had even completed pilot training I had seen a man who looked like Captain Stratton on television in what I knew later was a North Vietnamese film: the man was wearing a striped pajama suit of broad gray or black and white I thought.

In fact, the stripes were of broad maroon and gray, the likes of which I still had snapshots of Bryan wearing; at Kelly's insistence, he wore them now and then: at two years of age, she was fascinated with this outfit. Next to a vase of roses, the maroon rose buds and stripes looked to be in 3-D, with the red stripes and rose petals protruding to the front in those snapshots. The shoes were made from rubber tires, something always mentioned by Bryan when people would ask what it was like in the Hanoi Hilton, but not nearly as fascinating to Kelly as the striped prison pajamas.

In his prison stripes a man as tall, dark, and as imposing as Richard Stratton, even in these physical straits, had, in this television film clip, entered a small room seemingly made of concrete block, one in which he seemed too tall to stand. In fact, his arms were close at his sides and his hands were clasped together in front of him.

Stooped already, then he bowed. Another pilot, more wizened looking than the first, appeared from a door that looked Alice-in-Wonderland in size and went through the same motions. Then Jane Fonda stepped onto or into the screen's side; it appeared to be right there in Hanoi; speaking, she called them both and the rest of the pack in the back of the concrete-like looking sanctum, war criminals. She was mincing no words. Then, briefly, a group was shown playing basketball in the prison courtyard. Like waking from sleeping, I looked again and the pilots and Jane were gone from the screen.

In the years since the war I had envisioned, whenever her name was mentioned with regard either to her activities during the war or to her film making, meeting Jane Fonda. I had it planned in a lot of ways. I imagined engineering a meeting, holding her physically captive, and telling her off: I hated most what I thought of as her naivete on the subject of the war. Off-screen her sophistication would be diluted. I'd like to give it to her as she had been giving it to us, the American Public, in 1968 from Hanoi.

In the summer of 1985, I'd almost had my chance. I hadn't even planned it. I was visiting in the home of friends of my parents, Carol and Tom Ivanov. This was a summer vacation for me, and I had decided to go back to California. I missed it still; besides I could see Kelly, who was staying with Bryan in Los Angeles for the summer, for a week-end. Because I was going alone, my mother had suggested I stay the first night that I flew into Los Angeles with the Ivanovs. It turned out, they lived on Alta Street in Santa Monica and had lived there for thirty years before it became a street of movie stars. Theirs was a few houses north of Jane's on the same side of the street with Jane's being a few houses closer to the beach. Further down toward the beach, beyond her house, at the intersection of their street with Ocean Boulevard in Santa Monica, the beach lay at the foot of a steep green embankment which was part of the Santa Monica city park.

All of the Ivanov children had gone to Hollywood High School. Collectively, that was not the most unusual aspect about them. When they had still lived in San Anselo and we had visited them then, they had all been whiz kids. More whiz-kid-like than any of us. Now, their oldest son Steven was home for the summer too, and we all often took walks down toward the beach, going by Jane's on the way to and fro. In magazines, I had seen pictures of this very house, referred to by Jane herself as a modest place. What I noticed most was what it didn't have. For example, it didn't have a garage or even an alley of the sort found in older neighborhoods and which would have afforded some privacy of entrance. According to Mr. Ivanov, the limousines came right to the front curb, and in fact, we saw two, my very first day, do just that. It apparently didn't even much of a back yard, for that matter. And it didn't have a swimming pool. It was, in fact, a regular neighborhood of sorts.

The large houses were not unusually spaced. Jane's house was a two-story brick place, somewhat of a colonial style, and to my surprise one day walking, I found that it had a real mailbox, obscured by a huge front hedge. It was a plain black wrought iron box that was part of a very high wrought iron fence.

One afternoon coming back to the Ivanov's I saw Jane and a girl I realized must have been her own teen-aged daughter, come from inside their high gate and turn to walk toward the Santa Monica beach. Jane turned her head for some reason, looking back over her shoulder as I passed in my car going the opposite direction toward the Ivanov's. It seemed strange to me; it could hardly have been that she recognized the car as one belonging to the Ivanov's because this one was rented. It just happened, that was all. She waved at me, after looking at me directly as I pulled over to the curb, and she was smiling.

It truly was a Fonda smile. I smiled back. The rest of her I barely recognized because, for one thing, she was much smaller in real life than she seemed in the movies, and her simpleness in appearance, without make-up and without her hair done, didn't seem so different from that of the rest of us. Her daughter, whose hair was much darker, was about the same height as she, and the two went hurrying toward the beach for what seemed might be a late afternoon walk.

At its end, the street itself made a perpendicular with Ocean Boulevard high above the water; the Boulevard in its curves through Santa Monica ran parallel to a strip of park between the street level and the steep drop-off to the beach. In the late afternoon people jogged, bicycled, or simply strolled, just as they did elsewhere, only here they were minisculed beneath the enormous palms. Here too, at the end of the street where Alta ran into Ocean Boulevard, the corner was different from most: they said William Holden had died from falling in his high-rise apartment.

I got out of my car and peered down the street after Jane and her daughter. Down at the corner, the sun was setting; there the stoplight looked artificially placed, hung symmetrically in the very center of the setting sun. The fixture was small in the sun's center, and the sun, magnified in its setting was many-fold times larger than any object at the end of the street, save the palms and William Holden's apartment building. It appeared ready to sink beyond sight from the bank and beyond the reach of the rows of benches tilted against the sky. Some hundreds of feet above the ocean's level in the Santa Monica Park — down there at Alta and Ocean Boulevard — Jane and her daughter turned the corner out of sight.

Hurriedly, I walked the block to Jane's house and knocked on the gate. It only seemed greenly iridescent. With her out of the house, it was a good time to check it out. Up close the fence and gate were plain black wrought iron: it was the size of both that were overwhelming, inches and inches taller than I, making them substantially more than six feet; the gate part peaked higher, perhaps at seven feet, where the two halves came together in a single curve made by their meeting and it was affixed with a large black lock.

I looked for the wrought iron mailbox hidden to the left in the bushes. I knew it to be a part of the fence. Perhaps I should just write a note. I could always do that now that I knew she had a mailbox. I memorized the street number and pressed the buzzer that I found on the gate beneath the lock. A whirring noise came immediately from a camera completely hidden in the direction of the mailbox and apparently clicking my picture. Jane being out, I wondered if anyone would answer. A large black girl appeared behind the gate from nowhere. I hadn't seen her on the sidewalk from the door. Skin-glistening, she was implacable in appearance, perhaps for a purpose, I thought later. The camera whirring was either continuing or starting up again. I believed she only pretended not to understand me.

I talked anyway, asking her to tell Jane who I was, that I was visiting Mrs. Ivanov and that I would like to meet with her today or any day of this week to talk about POWs; I pointed up the street toward the Ivanovs: "Please tell her that it's important that I see her," I said. "Please have her call Mrs. Ivanov, 940 Alta, when she can." Again I pointed north on Alta. I said the telephone number aloud.

The girl turned and disappeared into the house; she had told me in brief reply that Jane was busy this evening. After dinner I walked past Jane's again and sure enough, a limousine that seemed as green and as iridescent as the gate from the distance, pulled up at the curb as I was step-ping up the same curb of her block at the corner. As I stopped in front, the driver told me without my prying, that he was picking up her daughter to take her to the airport to fly to Paris, and from further down the street, I watched them both come from the house. The same girl whom I had seen with Jane that afternoon walking toward the beach, climbed into the limousine.

Later that evening, while we all sat in the Ivanov's sun room watching TV, Kelly came hurrying in to say there was a movie star party going on down the block at Jane's. She wanted me to come and look. "It's dark out now, Mom," she said. "No one will even see you."

"I've been hanging around there all day," I commented. "Enough is enough. I didn't get to talk to her and doubt that she'll call me back, or that the girl will even tell her I came."

"Oh come on, Mom. Let's just go look. You've already seen her twice. I haven't even seen her once yet." She had heard nothing but bad things about Jane from Bryan, but her curiosity was overcoming her. I was still looking dubi-ously at her. We were all drinking lemonade and watching TV in the now near-dark. I was getting tired of the Jane Fonda subject. It was true, no one would have to see us hanging around again. Mr. Ivanov was on his feet already, and Steven and Mrs. Ivanov were laughing, urging us all to go on out. The three of us walked out, down toward Jane's, the third time for me this day.

Mr. Ivanov assured us that we could just be taking a walk. Then, we simply sat ourselves on the opposite curb for awhile. Jane's voice was easy to recognize, more star-tling somehow than her appearance, and it seemed to be coming from what was an upstairs balcony or the large sec-ond-story front window. In the daylight, in the center of the second story, I had noticed what was a multitude of small panes in a wall-sized window or perhaps a door. Now at night, on the second story, one could only see a center chandelier high in the ceiling and some peripheral lights above the huge front hedge that was almost invisible in the dark. The street cement and curb were still warm to the backs of our legs where we sat, but it was getting late; lim-ousines were pulling up. We listened as people began to leave and as they came outside and closer in leaving, try-ing to recognize any movie star voices in the dark, that we knew besides Jane's.

27

NATIONAL LEAGUE BY-LAWS

The afternoon business meeting was about to be called to order; on the platform were Colonel Brooks and Anne Mills Griffiths, the outgoing and incoming Executive Directors of the National League of Families, talking to one another. Now, in its sixteenth year of existence, the organization was founded by Sybil Stockdale as the National League of Families of American Prisoners and Missing in Southeast Asia. She had formed it out of the dilemma of the capture of her husband, Captain Jim Stockdale, the Navy pilot who was shot down in the Gulf of Tonkin and became the first POW.

This business meeting preceded the Sixteenth Annual Dinner in the evening, and the Closing Ceremonies' program of a Commemorative Candlelight Service would follow in the morning.

The members, despite its being directly after lunch, were talking animatedly among themselves on the main floor of the ballroom. I was surprised to see so many of the morning's participants in attendance of a business meeting. Now the Mark Plaza Ballroom was crowded, just as it had been this morning.

Again I saw the young woman who had spoken earlier at the CIL presentation. She was standing in the right - hand aisle across the ballroom. Finding my way through the crowd, I touched the girl's arm to gain her attention, and told her simply how much I had admired her speaking earlier, so calmly and so clearly.

"You won't regret it, no matter the outcome," I said, wondering myself why I made that comment.

The young woman herself looked confused for a moment, but pleased in any event. "Thank you so much," she responded and she talked again about how the information presented by the CIL showed a lack of specifics in identification procedures used for MIA remains. Then she said she would like for me, asking my name, to meet her sister whom she motioned to, some rows of wooden chairs toward the podium but whose blond resemblance was evident even at a distance.

The first girl's name was Laura, and her sister's name was Rachael. They lived across the river from each other in Kansas City, Missouri, and in Manhattan, Kansas. Their father had been an F-4 pilot stationed at Ubon, Thailand, when he was shot down and subsequently listed as missing.

I asked them together if they had ever talked to any other ex-POWs:

"Did you ever talk with the pilot who flew with your father when he was shot down?" They had already told me that the other pilot had lived through it, and had been captured.

"Not really," Rachael said.

"The reason I ask is that I just overheard another daughter, at least I assume she is a daughter in the back of the ballroom there as I came in, say she had just talked to a real POW. That was how she put it. She seemed very excited and glad. I heard her say also that it had helped her." The intervening years were welling up. Going on, I said, "When she spoke I remembered that all of you young people were very small children in 1973 when the war was ended and the POWs were released."

I went on. "Perhaps sometime you could find the pilots who lived with your father at the time in Ubon; I know Randolph Casualty Center would help you." I fell silent, knowing I had said much too much, wondering if Randolph Casualty still was in existence. But Rachael spoke quickly. "We do know one POW," she said. "You might know him. His name is Robert Garwood."

"Garwood?" I repeated it, thinking slowly. I'd heard his name, just his last name and never his first, when used by the POWs, "I don't understand," I said. "Surely I know of him, but the POWs don't count him among themselves."

I felt us all, Laura, Rachael, and myself as well, cringe as I said it. I tried to suck back the sentence with a breath inhaled; then I wanted to hug both girls to myself, to squeeze the air where the words hung between us, to nothingness. I could see my words, cartoon-like, in a shapeless bubble of jumbled letters in the air coming straight from my mouth. It was an awful swoop of words.

With enthusiasm Laura set out to correct me, never taking the least offense, for which I was grateful.

"Oh no," she said, "Those court martial charges are unfounded; his lawyer is here, right down the aisle." She gestured in the direction of the podium. "You should talk with him," and she pointed him out specifically. "There is a friend of mine you really should talk with — he really knows much more about this than I."

Laura took me by the arm and led me to a break in the rows of wooden chairs where a young man in a dark suit was sitting just beyond one of the microphones. She introduced us: it seemed he too was from Kansas City and was both a friend and a journalist.

"The truth is," Ken Howard began, "That many POWs did not live up to the military code of conduct. They all gave information to the North Vietnamese, and none of them is proud of his conduct."

He went on, and the girls and I stood silently without interrupting him. "Anything is forgivable under these circumstances, and many of the POWs say that Garwood's conduct was no better nor worse than their own."

The girls stood silent, but I heard myself saying no. Again no. "No, that's not the way it worked." Nor did I feel myself regretting the sentence.

"There were a very few — they were different from the rest — and the rest will not talk about them." I went on, "They lived differently in the prison camps from the rest of the air crew members. It is true that POWs will say they each gave information for which they were regretful, but Garwood and a few others were even different from them. Also, Garwood was not an air crew member. Those like Garwood, who were different, were considered so because of their cooperation with the North Vietnamese. They lived separately, they ate separately and and were not confined in the manner of the others. I understand from others in the camps, that they may have participated in the torture of the other prisoners."

I thought of the then recent front page article in the Wall Street Journal, citing Garwood repeatedly, as though he were a reputable source, concerning his own reports of live POWs still held in Vietnam. In the same month I'd seen his photo in another paper. He was positively a dead ringer, in the photograph, for the movie star, Jack Nickolson. I would have thought it to be Jack Nickolson but for the caption concerning the urging of the former POW,

Robert Garwood, to take a polygraph test. The wonderful leer of Jack Nickolson, no wonder in it. I had been thinking about Garwood a good bit this month. This was to have been my letter to the editor of the Wall Street Journal.

"Please don't listen just to me. You are all in your twenties now." I was looking at the surprise, more like shock, on the faces of all three, Laura, Rachael, and Ken, the young journalist. "You can ask for yourselves now." I kept going. "Ask," I said, "The POWs themselves. No one can tell you but them. My facts are questionable compared with theirs —- what I know is only second-hand. Ask them how they felt specifically about Garwood."

Bryan had told me about his stay in the Pig Stye, in pieces, from which I had made my own composite image. How, the last night in the dark they short-circuited the light socket to start a fire to cook the freeze-dried food from their U.S. packages, risking totally the well-being they did have: there — I imagine in the center of the compound's dark, free to move about — those Bryan had told me in his camp who were considered collaborators by the others.

"I think you'll find, in fact, that the majority of POWs found Garwood's conduct unconscionable, nor is his present conduct any more acceptable. I can give you the names and telephone numbers of some other POWs, if you like." The girls both said yes, again not taking offense at my verbiage, for which I was again grateful.

For some minutes Colonel Brooks had been trying to call the meeting to order to start the voting on resolutions put forth by various individuals and groups. Most of the fourteen resolutions were authored collectively by the regional divisions, each consisting of a geographical group of states. There were five of these such regional divisions of the League. The outcome of the voting was to be turned over to Congress, for their consideration in formulating policy concerning the POW/MIA issue. On the floor it appeared that voting members of the National League were to sit in the front middle section of rowed chairs, while those who were not strictly identified as members of the League were to sit in the side sections and the back middle section.

I told both girls that I had never become a proper League member, much as I had intended to do it many years ago. Eldora Ford had been a prime mover of the California National League group in the early 1970's, and I had intended to join it, but the war had ended within months of my even meeting and becoming friends with Eldora. Earlier in the day I had taken a form from a table outside the ballroom door to take home with the intention of becoming a member, that is if I would qualify now that Bryan and I were no longer married. But both girls poo-pooed my objections, all of my explanations, and they took me, each by an arm, off to the middle section telling Ken that I would be sitting with them. Just pleased that the girls wanted me to come along, despite my Garwood talk, I went willingly and gladly.

I looked at the sheaf of papers containing all the resolutions — Laura and Rachael each had a copy: Resolutions for Consideration - 16th Annual Meeting. A total of eleven resolutions was up for discussion and voting. Already it appeared that considering all the resolutions would take more time than was allotted on the program. The business meeting was to be concluded by 4:00. and it was 2:30 now, ninety minutes or eight minutes per resolution.

Nevertheless passage of the first three resolutions went smoothly and by voice vote. No one objected to calling upon the Government of the Socialist Republic of Vietnam to make a concrete proposal in negotiations with U.S. officials about any U.S. personnel still alive in Indochina; no one objected to extending their appreciation to Indonesian President Suharto and to his foreign minister, Mochtar Kusumaatmadja, for their aid in securing Vietnamese cooperation with the United States on this humanitarian issue, the Number One Resolution.

Some people objected to the Number Two Resolution that stated the National League should support lifting the Congressional ban on aid to Laos in an effort to improve the overall relationship between the U.S. and Laos. It was suggested that such improvement in relations would facilitate both the Pakse excavation and the gaining of information about the greater than 500 Americans still missing there. The resolution passed by a voice vote, following some rewording.

The next two resolutions, calling upon the People's Republic of China for an accounting for the six Americans still listed as missing and for access to Vietnamese refugees for the obtaining of information regarding these men, passed without objection.

Someone in the back then stood and made a motion that the group, due to a shortage of time, skip the next three resolutions and go directly to a consideration of Resolution Eight. Numbers Five and Six were resolutions urging one, the adoption of a National Prayer Program and two, that President Reagan continue the POW/MIA issue as one of highest national priority until a full accounting be obtained.

The group voted on these quickly and moved on to the eighth, by-passing No. 7. Both No. 7 and No. 8 were short; one looked like the inverse of the other. Resolution Seven had been passed already by Region III, consisting of the Washington D.C. environs, so one gathered from the discussion later, and had been unanimously supported by vote of the National League Board of Directors:

#7 RESOLVED, that the National League of Families oppose any effort by Congress to establish a commission or committee on the POW/MIA issue, in view of our confidence in the oversight capability of the Sub-Committee on Asian and Pacific Affairs House Foreign Affairs Committee, and the House POW/MIA Task Force and our strong support for "highest national priority" efforts now being implemented.

#8 RESOLVED, that the National League of Families strongly supports the Hendon Resolution concept to have another commission appointed to investigate the POW/MIA situation, but that it be comprised of those person, Congressional or otherwise, that H. Ross Perot decides he can work with.

Resolution 8 had been passed by Region I and opposed by a unanimous vote of the Board of Directors. Five individuals then spoke in succession using the left-hand microphone facing the podium: family members, two women and three men, all older than the girls I had spoken with. They would have to be counted as being more of my own age. They spoke in favor of the H. Ross Perot Commission, H. Ross Perot being the Texas billionaire who had who had taken POW wives around the world in pursuit of the release of POWs, and to Paris, for the Peace talks. He had founded Texas Instruments and was a billionaire and truly a philanthropist.

They said, all of these family members, that enough was enough, the U.S. Government hadn't, in fourteen years, gotten any accounting from the North Vietnamese for the 2,464 men about whom there still was little, if any, information. Let H. Ross Perot try it. If he couldn't do it, no one could, and they could accept it. Besides he was willing to take it on and he was a person who also did what he promised.

Then Ann Mills Griffiths herself stepped from the podium, down from the platform onto the ballroom floor and took the microphone. She couldn't have disagreed more, so she said. The U.S. Government was doing its best, there was a start, after all, to show an effort:

- the Pakse crash site was being excavated,
- the Laotian Government was indicating potential cooperation on future crash site excavations, and
- the North Vietnamese Government was indicating cooperation on B-52 crash site excavations around Hanoi.

"Showing a lack of confidence in the Reagan administration's efforts to Congress would just jeopardize future negotiations and future excavations." She went on to say, "What good would it do - only harm - to make a recommendation to Congress anyway? The National League is not a policy-making organization. We're only an organization of family members."

Laura now was on the opposite microphone in the right-hand aisle, calling for someone who was familiar with Robert's Rules of Parliamentary Procedure: "I would like to question the right of the moderator of this meeting to participate in debate on these resolutions," she was saying. Again I was astonished at her extraordinary calm. I hadn't seen her leave her chair and go to the microphone.

The meeting was beginning to degenerate. Ann Mills Griffiths, when no one rose to intercede with parliamentarian procedures, was followed by what appeared to be other adamant board members of the same position. I arose and went to the opposite microphone, where Laura was still standing.

I felt the base of it at my toes. Congress would, in fact, listen, to these families; there was little doubt, but clearly, they, the families, did not appreciate the extent to which other people did pay attention to them when they spoke. Maybe you had to be outside of it to see it. The American public would listen to the families themselves long after they quit listening to the politicians and to media-hype. Congress would also listen. There had, in fact, been no court martial of the B-52 pilot. On the one hand, I had never thought that my call to Senator Mathias had been the decisive factor in forestalling the court martial; on the other, I was persuaded that he had listened to me, and I had never heard or seen the court martial mentioned in the news after that day. The real point in the present was that the American public still held in respect families of the Missing-In-Action. The microphone, in my hands, was as cold and slick as any I had ever held.

Colonel Brooks, still on the platform, addressed me: "I see miss, that you do not have a name badge. Would you please identify yourself."

"I'm sorry, I came late and I did not know that it was necessary to register. My name is Layne Martin and I am from Michigan."

"I'm sorry," said the Colonel, "But you must be identified as a family member or have some relationship to the POW/MIA situation."

I spoke again. "I apologize for my lack of a nametag, I did not know."

"I'm sorry, miss," the Colonel went on before I could continue. "But I cannot allow you to speak."

I interrupted the Colonel, "My name is Layne Martin. I was married to a POW, and I think I have a right to speak."

"We cannot give you permission, I'm sorry."

The colonel and I were clearly finished, there was no way around it. I had to abide by it; short of contributing more to the parliamentary disarray, there was no choice. I let the mike slip and turned back to my seat. Laura and Rachael hugged me hard. I told them goodbye, and as though all part of one motion, in order to be able to do it, I boarded a busload of MIA mothers and road to the Vietnam Memorial; I found John and Michael's names; they were together, chronologically the end of the war: left slab, bottom right at the inside crevice where the two slabs meet. I rode back to the hotel, grateful to be with the mothers. They were very quiet in their collective anguish; I, for the moment, was safe in my own because I was with them. At the hotel, I found a cab to the airport, and I flew back to Michigan.

28

ALMS FOR OBLIVION

When two people suffer the death of a third, particularly if the third occurs out of the normal order of things, as with a child or a sibling, or one might say, as with a friend in war, the consequences may occur in one of two ways. Following an initial inevitable collision between the two, either those two people will become one completely, absorbing the death between them and leaving no space between for a demise by the visage of the third; or, failing such, those two may bounce off of one another, even unto the ends of the earth. And it may be that they shall never meet again.

SCIENTISTS SAY ARMY LIED IN
ATTEMPT TO CLOSE MIA CASES

by Gregory Spears
Free Press Washington Staff

"WASHINGTON —Several experts who have examined records detailing how the Army went about identifying the remains of 13 Americans missing in action during the Vietnam War contend that the Army deliberately misinterpreted evidence in order to claim that it had identified the victims.

"Suspicions about the Army's methods first were raised last year by a scientist who were asked to examine bone fragments returned to relatives for burial. He contended that the Army's methods included unsound leaps in judgment to hastily establish conclusive identification of the victims.

"But after examining the Army's records, which previously had not been available to outsiders, several forensic scientists have concluded that only deliberate distortions could explain why the Army made fundamental mistakes in its identification methods.

"A Defense Department spokesman strongly denied the allegations.

"The scientists — all experts in identifying human

remains — say the Army drew unwarranted and far-reaching conclusions about height, weight, sex, and age from bone fragments — and, in one case, identified what actually was a skull fragment as a piece of pelvic bone.

"These conclusions are just totally beyond the means of normal identification, our normal limits, and even our abnormal limits,' said Dr. William Maples, curator of physical anthropology at the Florida State Museum. Maples said that rather than being able to identify 13 sets of human remains — as claimed by the Army — he could not be certain of more than four.

"Added Dr. Michael Charney, emeritus profession of anthropology at Colorado State University who has examined the remains of the 13 missing men identified by the Army, 'I think it's a case of distortion.'

"The Anthropologists' criticism is focused on the Army's contention last July that it had identified the remains of 13 MIAs from bone fragments gathered at a crash site in the Laotian jungle. All 13 servicemen were aboard an Air Force AC130A gunship shot down during a night combat mission on Jan. 21, 1972.

"Several families of those aboard the plane have thought that some of the 13 survived the crash. Five open parachutes and piles of bloody bandages were found near the site.

"Ten families accepted the remains and buried them. The other three families asked Charney and another forensic anthropologist to check the identifications. In two of the three cases, the experts said they could not support the Army's identification.

"But their findings have buttressed broader accusations by POW-MIA organizations that the military is falsifying identifications to account for as many Vietnam-era MIAs as possible in an effort to close its books on that war. Said Donald Parker of Beaverton, Oregon, the nephew of an MIA, 'I think we have an attitude saying "These are the remains, we know they are these people — let's identify them."

"However, a Defense Department spokesman strongly denied these allegations, declaring that the Reagan administration is seeking a "full and complete accounting" of the 2441 Americans unaccounted for in Southeast Asia.

" 'I would find any allegations of intentional distortions...to be totally absurd,' said Lt. Col. Keith Schneider.

"Charney, of Colorado State, sparked a furious debate among his colleagues at the annual meeting of the American academy of Forensic Sciences in New Orleans last month when he contended that the Army's errors in identifying the AC130A's victims were so glaring that they must have been intentional.

" 'I think he's done a very thorough job, ands he's looked at the evidence more closely than anyone else.' Gill said.

"Many at the conference accused him of criticizing the Army too harshly. But George Gill, professor of anthropology at the University of Wyoming, said he has examined Charney's evidence and agrees with him.

"Charney was asked by relatives of the victims to look at three sets of remains to confirm the Army's identification - and says he has found serious mistakes in all three.

"In one case Charney reviewed, the Army said it used a fragment of pubic bone - part of the human pelvis - to establish age, and then identified it and other bones as the remains of James Ray Fuller, an Air Force chief mast sergeant of the same age who was on the flight.

"But according to Charney, 'It was not pubic bone at all. It was a bone from a skull. And even if it had been a pubic bone,' Charney added, 'The fragment had none of the characteristic ridges necessary to enable a scientist to determine its age.'

"Said Gill, 'In the case of Mr. Fuller, no matter how much benefit of the doubt you give the Army forensic anthropologist, there are some things there that point very strongly at intellectual dishonesty.'

"In another case, Army records show that the victim's height was estimated from a fragment of the humerus, or upper arm bone - which then was identified as the remains of the man close closest in height of those aboard the plane who had not been identified.

"However, Charney said his inspection of the arm bone fragment shows it was broken off above the depression that Army scientists have used as one of three landmarks to calculate the victim's height.

" 'He said he measured to the tip of the depression,' Charney said, 'But it wasn't there. It was broken away.'

"Maples, the Florida museum curator, said that in

many of the 13 cases, the Army used cranial sutures - the jagged lines where portions of the skull are knit together - to determine age. But he said the whole skull - not the small fragments used by the Army - is needed to make an accurate assessment of age."

To: Mr Gregory Spears
Detroit Free Press Washington Staff

Dear Mr. Spears:

I am writing to you with regard to your recent Detroit Free Press article, *In Search of the Missing*. In that article about Vietnam which specifically concerned the military's identification of crew members' remains found at the crash site of an AC130 gunship in Laos, you quoted allegations made by three of the thirteen families involved that identifications made on the bone fragments found at the site were questionable. You also cited corroborating findings by nonmilitary forensic anthropologists with reference to these three sets of remains, as reported at the American Academy of Forensic Scientists' meetings in January of this year.

In this article there were repeated allusions to the military's involvement as being performed by the Army. In fact, there are seventeen allusions to the Army. I refer specifically to the Army's identification of the remains of the thirteen members of the AC130 crash site. Although it is neither here nor there, a moot point to you perhaps, I would like to point out an error in that it was the Air Force, not the Army that was involved.

This was an Air Force AC130 gunship, as it is called, and hence it carried Air Force crew members (see paragraph seventeen for your own reference to the

Air Force Chief Master Sergeant).   The site of the military forensic anthropology laboratory is at Clark Air Force Base in the Philippines, and the remains that were refused by Donald Parker of Beaverton Oregon, nephew of an MIA, as the article states, were returned to the Air Force officials who delivered them. So you see, Mr. Spears, this was an Air Force, and not an Army, gig.

Sincerely,
Layne Martin

To: Tom Wolfe
Author, THE RIGHT STUFF

Dear Mr. Wolfe:
    For some time now, in fact since four years ago Thanksgiving Day, I have been thinking about writing to you with regard to your then recent book, THE RIGHT STUFF. Since then, as you know, a movie has been made, featuring my favorite star, Sam Shepard, and the story of Chuck Yeager has become one of American storytelling renown.
    You are to be commended for bringing his story and the lives of those like him to life. My one question, however, with the book has to do with your definition of *The Right Stuff*. The analogy of "The Little Indians," Chapter Seven, I found confusing. You'll remember the Navy pilots lined up in their peacoats for the funeral of a fallen (so to speak) comrade pilot-friend. I gather by *The Right Stuff* in that situation you were referring, rather uncomplimentarily, to the inability of the other classmates in their pilot training class, the seven or so attending, to comprehend, that is accept in a straight-forward manner, the death of

their classmate. On your unpretty pre-
sumption of some conscious or uncon-
scious non-acknowledgment of the risk
of flying and its consequences on the
part of these pilots, you stated they were
then able to climb back into their Navy
cockpits. Correct me if I'm wrong. In
fact, Mr. Wolfe, you alluded to those
Indians in their peacoats seventeen
times in that one chapter. So I do con-
clude that you were rather promulgating
us with this analogy. My thought is that
your thought is that military pilots are
not very bright. In this regard, there is a
recent reference that might be relevant,
called IN LOVE AND WAR by Jim and
Sybil Stockdale. You'll perhaps remember Jim Stockdale, if not as a POW, then
as a recent Vice-Presidential Candidate.

Let me quote the Stockdale reference for you. I should preface the quote
by saying that the Vietnam POWs had a
tap code by which they communicated.
(And I guess information just rippled
from room to room and camp to camp).
Stockdale quotes a new prisoner: 'You
know, the code and how you use it is all
written out on the bottom of the quiz
table in the knobby room. I spent my
first night in Hanoi tied up on the tor-
ture-room floor. I looked up at the bottom of that table and there some Yank
had written - "All American Prisoners
Learn This Code." '

I wouldn't want you to think I'm
being melodramatic or anything, but you
see, Mr. Wolfe, I think there may be some
quality you are missing in these military
pilots, however respectable past partici-
pation in the Vietnam War may seem to
you now. I know these guys fly and fly
and fly, and they never use the word die,
I'm sure you said that somewhere in your

book whether I read it or not (in fact, they call it buying the farm), but I think they know about it, more or less, even if they never use the word. Certainly more than you or I anyway, even if they do keep going, i.e., flying, right down to the end, so to speak, of the line. Like the guys on the AC130 that crashed in Laos that Mr. Spears just wrote about. I saw some guys go to Guam and to Thailand so they could fly combat over Vietnam, and they were quite sure they wouldn't come back, and they didn't either. They knew. I'm just trying to say I think you may be in error there. As a matter of fact, Tom, I'm thinking of the ELECTRIC-KOOL-AID ACID TEST. I just think you may have somewhat of a credibility problem.

I know a couple of pilots, needless to say, not as famous as Chuck Yeager, but they have seen him from afar on some flight line, and they know guys who have flown with him, and they say "the right stuff" is a bunch of baloney. I even think Mr. Yeager himself said, on the back of the book jacket, that he didn't know what it was. It's not that that bothers me. In fact, I think there may be something to the right stuff thing myself and maybe those guys don't know it because they have it.

It's just that I read the EKATest in 1972, when the Vietnam War was pretty much at a peak. As a matter of fact, I was living alone because the guy I was living with was busy bombing S.E. Asia. Now I've let the cat out of the bag, and you'll say I have a credibility problem too. But I don't write books, you see. My problem with your work is that you wrote EKATest and then you turned around and wrote THE RIGHT STUFF. I know no one uses the word radical anymore but we did

then (about you certainly, your dis-
claimer to being an impartial journalist
notwithstanding). Surely you remember
Eldridge Cleaver, in California, a main
man of the radicals. To be honest, I'd
have as hard a time   imagining Mr.
Cleaver in a three-piece suit, fact that it
is today, as I do trying to imagine you
writing THE RIGHT STUFF (also a fact). I
certainly wouldn't want to use the word
opportunistic to describe your literary
achievements although frankly I'd have
found the impartiality you claim as a
journalist better touted had you written
them out-of-step with their times, like in
the opposite order: the one then, and
the other, now. I just think, begging your
pardon, I'd have done better with your
literary achievements if you had just sort
of stuck to your "EKATest-Kandy-
Kolored-Tangerine-Flake-Sreamline-
Baby-Radical-Chic-&-Mau-Mauing-the-
Flak-Catchers" guns right down to the
end, so to speak, of the Pump-House-
Gang-Line.

Sincerely,
Layne Martin

To: Jane Fonda
402 Alta, Santa Monica, CA

Dear Jane:
       A year or so ago I was in Santa
Monica staying in the block next to your
own with friends of my parents, and this
summer I am planning to come to
California again for a visit. Since I will
be staying a few days with these friends
(The Ivanovs) (four doors north of you), I
thought that I would write ahead to see
if you might find a time which might be
convenient for us to have tea together.

You see when I knocked on your gate last summer I was remembering the night my friend Eldora thought she heard you coming in her window after her. We always rather assumed that it really was you. I'd best explain. You remember the Vietnam War, I'm sure. Please forgive my maligning your perspicacity, but I'd gathered that was one you would just as soon forget.

You and my friend Eldora, as it turns out, were on television in Sacramento on the same day in the winter of l973 during February, the middle month of the POW return, a day you happened to come to town for a television appearance and one on which Eldora was being simultaneously interviewed regarding the POWs & MIAs, fortunately on another station. I say it was fortunate because Eldora's husband was a POW, a very old shootdown, and she had worked very hard for their return, that is for the release of all of the POWs, and she didn't appreciate your calling them war criminals (the implication being apparently that we should let them sit tight right there in Hanoi or wherever). In all fairness, she didn't think you appreciated her calling you names either. So, when a window happened to fall down in the middle of the same night, you'll understand I'm sure, she thought it might be you, Jane, coming in after her.

I'm going to have to hurry now, as I've already written a number of letters this evening on the subject of Vietnam, and I'm a little tired of the whole thing. I know you've had a hard time yourself — I'm serious — Fonda movie star or no, so I try not to be hasty in my judgment. I know you've been married to

Tom Hayden and that he is quite respectable now. We all are. I mean, who even remembers the Chicago Seven. Kids these days have never even heard of them. Now Tom's in a three-piece suit, no less, so I saw on the Ivanov's coffee table in that brochure for his campaign for the California Legislature or the Santa Monica City Council, I can't remember which.

I do have some trouble with that, I admit, like I said in my letter to Tom Wolfe earlier this evening, about going from writing the ELECTRIC KOOL AID ACID TEST to THE RIGHT STUFF via some mental whoosh I don't under-stand. But my thought is that maybe if you and I, Jane, could have tea in the shade on yours, or Mrs. Ivanov's, patio - either one, I could stop thinking about you, I mean about hanging on your gate, waiting forever, last summer, for you to come out.

Sincerely,
Layne Martin

To: Mrs. Ellen Dearborn

Dear Ellen,

This is not a fictitious letter, nor is it one written from the asylum. I am alive and well enough, and I mean for this to be a real letter. Properly speaking, I should obtain your address and send this to you through the regular mail.

I am writing to you about John and about what has happened to all of us since 1972 of the crew's being shot down and John's being listed as MIA. I could say that I wasn't able to obtain your address, but of course, that isn't entire-ly so. I know that I could find you no matter what it took to do it; it would be possible. I can say that I have been to Washington to the National League of Families' office, that I have the card of someone there, and were I to cite it at Randolph Casualty, someone might give me your address even though I am no longer associated with the Air Force. I know that Mr. Ferro, of the Defense Intelligence Agency, whose card I also obtained in Washington, might help me locate you. I know your families lived in Pinehurst, North Carolina, and I know you moved that summer, to Seattle. I could go to both places, and somehow find out how to find you. Surely it is clear to you, by now, that I am afraid to do so. Both for reasons having to do with you and for reasons having to do with me.

I am sorry, Ellen, for not being there all these years. I don't quite know how it happened that you and Bryan and I now are spread across the country, likely at the three furthest distances possible: east to west coasts, when in fact, we should have given our best to survive together. After his return and John's non-return, and how we had hoped he would just show up —Bryan knew he was alive the night they took him in — you just disappeared. We didn't stop you and we didn't follow you. Now, for the three of us, you and me and Bryan, avoiding one anothers' reflections, I don't think, has helped us make it through. We all should have taken care of the children together, raised them and sent them to school, and we should have truly helped each other through. It has been 20-plus years since then, December, 1972. I should never have lost you from my life. And we, Bryan and

I, should have been there to help John's mother before she died and John's brother too. When we flew East that August, we should have been going to North Carolina, not to Nixon's dinner. I knew that at the very time that we did it.

I am sorry, Ellen. Never, in my life, have I failed anyone as I have failed you. My trepidations are what keep me hiding in the crowd. How will I find you and how will you find me. I don't know that you are still alive and well. I am afraid to find out; in fact, I crouch here in the crowd, watching for this to be printed, as I am sure that much will happen, and I know that I will be amidst both jeers and cheers, but all of it will keep me hidden like some animal-critter, low along the ground with everyone around me shouting — something. I am in the process of finding the courage to stand up.

Sincerely,
Layne

Postscript
To:
the Senate Select Committee on POW/MIA Affairs
the Defense Department
the Defense Intelligence Agency
the National Security Council
the White House

Re:
The 1994-revealed
1200 North Vietnamese photos
of air crews and air crash sites

More than bones
There was a youth from Tampa's vicinity
Whose father was likened to Santini;
Known well as a swashbuckler,
A Navy pilot and father,
One thing he was not, was a weenie.

Now the youth to the Hill did travel;
His purpose was there to unravel
His father's mysterious,
Inexplicable disappeareance:
A Senate committee come under the gavel.

When the days wound down in testimony,
The youth, given over to parsimony,
Said little concerning
His own youthful yearning;
Instead, he gave facts of a larceny.

The photo-exhibit he gave the committee
Did add to the data substantially;
An aircraft capsule and number,
No bones were found under
Let the Gov't lock it back for posterity.

An ejection capsule unbroken!
The words go unspoken;
For the Senate to acknowledge
A father likely in bondage
Is too much, give that lad his mere token.

Now in Alexandria where Senators reside
They say a Headless Horseman does ride:
A pilot and compatriot,
Great Santini's real favorite,
The son on his saddle astride.

All may be true, whispers he of the bones
Of other pilots who never came home,
But I will remind you
Forever I'll find you;
Alive then, I'll haunt you down now alone.

epilogue

The figure is minute in the distance with heat waves as fluid and as tangible as water melting and reforming over the asphalt beneath the pilot's feet. One needs binoculars really to see that distance, out across the runway, the rows of camouflaged F-4s, and on to the hanger, all fading together in the afterburner heat and haze behind the pilot, carrying his helmet underneath his arm and finishing one more day of training.

The sun is golden, a huge preposterous parasol hung high over the Mojave Desert, some eighty miles above Los Angeles. A Southern California sand city, on the road straight to Las Vegas. There is a stillness in the midst of motion, a moviereel that has lost its soundtrack, and superimposed, the absolute roar that is deafening, literally, of F-4s, the Air Force's most reliable fighter, taking off and landing again, touch and goes they call them, on the runway of George Air Force Base, rehearsing then for Vietnam, if you will, in the summer of 1969.

And in the spring of 1972, March 30, this time in Northern California, Travis Air Force Base, the last MAC planeload of POWs lands. The American flags in the sunlight are dizzying to the crowds waiting. A last figure, minute again in the distance, disembarks. And one knows, that is I know, that there is more of a connection between 1969 and 1972 than of the figure I see.

I would hide in the San Gabriel Mountains that I have lived behind or the Sierra, running between those two Air Force bases, melt them right down and cover myself with them if I could, in order to avoid understanding it. For the present, I cannot drive Route 99, behind the Sierra running California north to south or south to north, not yet, its midpoint the B-52 departure base, Merced Air Force Base, for flight to Guam; and Guam, a daily mission departure point for Vietnam. Route 99, straight through the San Joaquin valley town of Merced equals the road of true doom I drove for two men at midnight of a Christmas Eve.

So now I drive 101 closer to the coast, unfamiliar in its route, but comforting in its sun-scorched mountain-hills, laden with live oak. Even as I do so, I know that I cannot drive the coast enough times to tread down the events of California.

Surely it is true, I did not fight or fly in Vietnam; I was in no position of danger. But I watched it up close, closer than television. I understand now that for me, I think for some more than just myself, the veil of Vietnam is still in California: its feel more real there than what we know as the Vietnam War could or ever would seem in the jungle-land of Vietnam itself for those of us who were never there, more real for me than a slick navigation map of S.E. Asia in all of its detail in a pile of flying gear or, nightly television, even in 3-D.